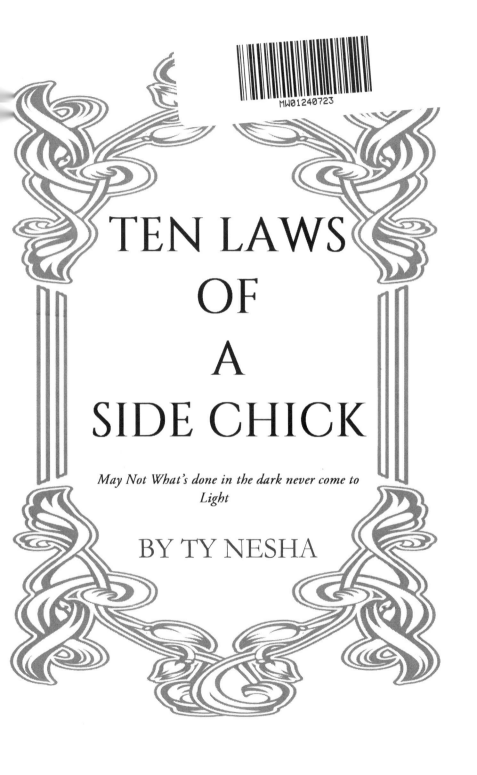

TEN LAWS
OF
A
SIDE CHICK

May Not What's done in the dark never come to Light

BY TY NESHA

Book and Cover design by Navi' Robins for NS Graphic Studios
www.nsgraphicstudio.com

ISBN:
First Edition: Febuary 2022
10 9 8 7 6 5 4 3 2 1

INTRODUCTION

It takes two to tango!

efore I begin, I am not condoning, glorifying, or uplifting "side chicks" in any way, shape, or form. However, I am not here to judge either. Side chicks and side chick-ism has been around since the creation of man. Let me present to you the history of "side chicks and concubines." Many people do not know that some prominent men of God in the Bible had concubines, also known as the current idiom for Side chicks or Mistresses.

Society paints side chicks as homewreckers or philandering. But side chicks are individuals too, and they're not always evil beings. After all, love is complicated. These side chick stories might make you see them in a different light. Being someone's side chick doesn't mean you don't have a heart. Some get into being the other woman unknowingly while others venture into it deliberately for monetary favors, and it also works for people who have commitment issues.

The perception of the "other woman" or the other man" occurs when two individuals participate in a relationship that doesn't require commitment. This relationship sustains while one or both are committed to other people. This relationship can be interchangeable and purposeful for many reasons, including sexual, emotional, or even transactional.

Over time and in many generations, individuals from either gender have handled infidelity to their own understanding, whether to turn a blind eye or become more accepting of the side chick position for various purposes.

Every individual has their own story that justifies their roles, and when it comes to dating, connections, and love, there are no guarantees and no conditions. After all, love is considered to be unconditional.

No man or woman is adultery-proof, and no one woman or one man is verified to be "un-fuck-wit-able!"

When it's all said and done, it takes two to tango!

Thus, without further ado, here are the top 10 rules that sidepieces must know

His woman:

You will never be his wifey!

His side:

Well, we all can't be the Queen B. I'll take the perks; you can have the extra baggage.

PROLOGUE

"For if the laws are broken, thou shall burn in the pits of side chick hell. Ashes to ashes, dust to dust, to all unruly side chicks."

 sat at the head of the table, sipping on my Amaretto Sour swaying to the music. I leaned back in my seat as each of the ladies strolled their way into the room with their heads hung low, looking for some level of empathy that I just wasn't about to hand out.

"What you in for?" One of the girls asked the other.

"The second law." She mumbled. "You?"

"Five...but...."

"Damn bitch, I know you lying!" One of the others intervened, popping her lips and rolling her eyes.

"Enough!" I shouted, disgusted at the very sight of each one of these chicks.

I stood to my feet, placed both hands on the table, and leaned in, speaking slow and clear.

"You Bitches are actually sitting here comparing failures? Did you forget how this game is played, or did you decide to play the game your way?

Either way, you got the game completely fucked up, and I say this with the utmost disrespect!"

I stood tall and lit the fire, shaking my head at the sight of them. These hoes broke every rule, disregarded every law, and threw the whole damn side chick bible out the window.

Each law was put into place, not to promise perfection, but to serve as a handbook for the side chick's well-being and know their place and not get the game twisted. Somewhere along the line, side chicks forgot that they were just that, The Chick on the Fucking Side of the game!

Side chicks from all over deemed to exalt the throne above the shines of the main. Consequently, they were cast out of *Side chick Paradise* and into the sides of the pits of Hell.

In a nutshell, side chicks got comfortable and out of their bodies because they were prideful and wanted the glory of the throne.

"Burn in Hell Bitches!

Ashes to ashes and dust to dust to you entitled ass, unruly side chicks." I scoffed, tossing the fire into the group. I watched each one of them turn to dust in pleasure as I thought back to the time, the day, hell, the minute I signed the contract to be the woman to another woman's man…

LAW ONE
Thou Shall Respect the Game

"When her time was up, she did not saunter in shadows or plead for more time. She placed the deck on the table and exited the game with grace."

Have an Exit Plan 1:1-2

The Goddess "The Successful Side Chick"

Game Over!

he crowd was mild, and the mood was chill. Just how I liked it. I needed this like yesterday. I was tired of the bullshit of the past trailing into my tomorrow. I just needed to breathe, if only for a moment.

"Can I get you a drink?" The baritone voice sent chills down my spine, straight to the heart of my femininity.

"I'm good, thanks," I spoke over the music, bobbing my head up and down to *50-Cents*, "Candy Shop." This man's scent danced around my nostrils, making me want to give him every bit of the candy I had in this here sugar bowl; don't judge, it's been a while.

His expensive cologne wasn't the only thing turning me on. It was everything for me.

"You know what? Why not." I smiled cunningly. Needless to say, one drink led to…

 opened one eye as the sun radiated through the hotel window. He sat at the edge of the bed, body glistening, saturated with my juices.

"I enjoyed you, all of you." He spoke over his shoulder while pulling his shirt over his head.

"Is that right?" I smiled, picturing the most vivid moments of the night before.

"It is, but…"

"The only time I wanna hear *but* is when the sound of mines is clapping to the rhythm of your…"

"Listen, I'm digging you. I really am, but… I mean, it's just, I got a lady at home and…"

"And that has absolutely nothing to do with me." The words escaped from my mouth before my brain could catch up.

Did I mean to say that? Was the penis so good that I was willing to play "the backup"? Where in the entire fuck was that self-respect I was telling Chanel about?

If I didn't mean that shit, this was the time for me to mean every word.

"So, what are you saying? You cool with that?" He raised his brows and scanned my face for an expression. My tongue danced around my lips, tasting the intricate components of his flesh from the night before.

"As I said, the only thing I'm worried about is what position you want me in before you walk out that door. Anything else ain't got nothing to do with me."

2

Right then, right there, I knew what choice I was making, and I also knew the contract I had just signed. As a matter of fact, I signed that paper in print, cursive, and in a language that only he and I would understand.

<hr>

"There something on your mind I can see right through you; I know your girl been treating you wrong… she ain't no good for you…" *Dmx* and *Monica's* "Don't Gotta Go Home" serenaded my ears as my lips met his. He cuddled up against me, laying his head in my bosom.

After six months of this, I never got tired of him. I listened, he vented, all while taking my tongue on a round trip vacation up and down his body. The more he let out the woes of his world, the harder I worked to relieve his tension. Knowing my role, I played it well, almost too well.

He never had to hear of me being too tired. When the "time of the month" came around, there were always two holes left. If he was frustrated, I threw it back, no back talk, none of that, and the only time I gave him hell was when he wasn't fucking me hard enough. There was no such behavior as smacking my lips or storming off when she called.

Most of you are reading this, sucking your teeth, and thinking, *"don't you know you are worth more than that? You do realize he is never going to leave her for you, don't you?"*

Let me say this. The side chick life isn't for everybody. You look at the side chick and sum her up to be just another soft chick with no morals, standards, or a clue, for that matter. If I say so myself, the game isn't for the weak.

In all actuality, a proper side chick is no such thing. That's you new age, wanna be relevant ass side chicks. You come with a sense of entitlement that doesn't even belong to you in the first place; you never did and never will. You hard-headed ass chicks are the sole reason for me writing these laws.

In my case, my worth has been deemed, and I knew two things for sure, I expected nothing from him and slept very well at night, not having some random bitch coming to me as a woman. And when the jig was up, I knew when to cash out!

I knew that catching feelings were dangerous and a one-way trip to *"Hey Barbara, this is Shirley"* phone calls that left me holding on to the line while they trailed off into the wind to do this shit all over again.

"So, you mean to tell me you don't love him? I mean, you are with him, damn near every day. Hell, if anybody should be the side chick, it's her. How do you even do it?" My girl Candy asked sincerely.

"Love him? No. I enjoy him. And he enjoys me as well."

"Well, do you love ya self? I mean damn sis; you do realize you are nothing more than an easy lay, right?" My other friend Brittany scoffed.

She had just caught her man cheating yet again, and I wasn't her favorite person in the world at this time.

"I love myself very much, Brittany! So much that I explore every part of me on a daily. So much that I choose when and how I deal with a man, let me ask you a question: Do you love yourself? I mean, it's only the fifth time you have caught Brandon dipping off, and each time you went straight after *her*, never holding *him* accountable."

"That's because these hoes know about me, and when you mess with another woman's man, you get exactly what's coming to you."

"Interesting, because if you expect her to respect you and his relationship, you will forever be doomed. My loyalty doesn't lie with a bitch I only hear about in between breaths of him coming up for air. Complaining about how she isn't who she used to be.

I am his peace, not to make him leave her, but because I'm at peace with the fact that he's not worth much more than a 'lay' and a good nut. Maybe some deep conversation that doesn't involve him having to sensor a damn thing.

He confides in me and never has to worry about me throwing shit in his face because he isn't my problem. He's hers. In addition, he

4

overcompensates, showering me with gifts and affection because every minute he's away from me, he feels like I'm neglected. If I can flip a coin and could choose to be on your side or the side I'm on, sis, I choose to stay here."

"So, forget her feelings, huh? Do you even have a heart, sis?"

"Listen, it's nothing personal. I'm doing her a favor. When she is too tired, I'm not! So, he doesn't pressure her. He doesn't complain when she doesn't cook because I already fed him. I give him tips on talking to her and teaching him how to make love to her by letting him fuck me.

The best part of it all is that I can send him on his way because he is not my issue, and I have no plans to insert myself into a position of being his full-time anything. I didn't sign a contract with, nor do I owe any form of loyalty to anyone other than myself." I said in a matter-of-fact tone.

"So that makes it right? What about karma? Do you believe in that at least?"

"Is it right? Maybe not? But it's right for me, right now! I understand that this is not long-term and that there is no room for hopes of happily-ever-afters here. As for karma, that bitch visited me before I even became a side chick. You simple-minded bitches kill me, trying to guilt-trip her into feeling guilty and continue to give him the luxury of keeping you. Where is his karma, huh?"

She parted her mouth to speak, but I put up my hand to silence her, "with that being said, I respect the game, play my position, and know when it's time to throw in the towel." I chuckled, looking at the large diamond on my finger.

"My Karma is me choosing me every time! My karma is choosing that if a man can't give me his all, I make the rules and play the game my way. I would never wife him; yea, you heard It right. He ain't long-term worthy. It's not my fault her man broke the rules and fell in love with me; meanwhile, I upgraded to someone ready to give me the world and more."

I emerged from my seat and threw my bag over my shoulder. "My time is up, win, lose or draw. She can have him; my exit will be quiet and drama-free!"

I grabbed my dear friend by the face cupping her cheeks, bringing her eyes up to mine. "You have to know when to stop allowing people to play games with your heart. Show them the difference between the player and the game. You are the fucking game! Pull the board off the table and leave him with the pieces.

Game Over!"

DAILY READ

I cannot advise on anything that I haven't experienced myself. How foolish would that be to do such a thing? Yet, I come before you today with the gems of a successful piece to his puzzle.

Many of you side chicks wonder why you will never be more than a thorn in his side and will not retire from this game properly. You stay far beyond your expiration date, spoiling his appetite, and is left starving for attention and validation. You become dick-matized and thrown off course, forgetting that you never were the main course in the meal.

The game is to be sold, not told; a side chick must respect the game and what it represents. The way this game would go is solely up to the way it is played, and the most cardinal rule is always to know when you sign that contract...

You are number two! Never forget that!

In every game you play, there are levels. As the Goddess, I performed the game like a Violinist at the arena. I played my hand, knew my position, and knew when to exit. If you don't respect this game, don't play it! This game comes with a shelf life. It is not meant to be long-term; the longer you stay in it, the more disastrous it becomes. Don't be like the dope boy on the corner that never had an exit plan. All side chicks must have an exit plan.

Side chick affirmation of the day!

Say this aloud and repeat it!
"I will respect the game and play my role."
Side chick-alations:
1

LAW TWO
Thou Shall not Falleth in Love

"The feelings of a side chick will never take precedence over the Queen that holds the throne."

Get out of your feelings 2:1

Daphne "The Vulnerable Side Chick"
You have the ball, but it's not your court!

I sat at my window, twirling my finger around my cup of coffee. I had cleared my entire schedule for Donald, and he had done the same for me. Today was our two-year mark of seeing one another, and what an incredible two years it has been.

I met Don at a party on my 30th birthday. He and his military buddies were invited to the after-party at my place. He sat in the club's back incognito with his brim hat, a pair of Levi's, and a crisp button-up. We talked the whole night as if no one else was in the room but us.

At the time, I wasn't looking for anything serious. My divorce was finalized two weeks prior, and after a decade of being locked down, I

9

just wanted to be free.

"So, what's your story?" I asked, holding the phone as the broad smile spread across my face.

"Well, I've been in the military for almost ten years. A sergeant for two and a half, and I have a three-year-old baby girl."

His strong southern accent aroused me.

I sat up from my comfortable position and cleared my throat. "Isn't that precious. Her mother?" I pried.

"My wife." He asserted.

"Oh! You're married?"

"Yes, for six years now, she is also in the military."

I grew silent.

"Is that a problem for you?" He asked.

"No, not a problem. I don't mind having a new friend. Nothing more." I affirmed.

Over time, Don and I grew closer; he was always there with a listening ear, and whenever I needed anything, he had my back. I made it very clear that everything about this friendship was platonic, nothing more, nothing less. I wasn't in the business of sharing a man, and I damn sure wasn't about to get struck by God himself by sleeping with someone's husband.

Donald's wife was always away, and he and I grew closer by the days. Six months ago, we took things to another level.

"Donald, you will never believe what he did now?" I vented to Donald about the horrid adventures of co-parenting. He always calmed my spirit and eased my soul.

"Let's take a ride." He offered.

Donald and I went on lots of dates. We were in public together many times, and our friendship wasn't at all a "secret." At least not to us. I respected his marriage, but after a while, things changed. Feelings grew, and my limitations were lifted.

He leaned into me, planting his soft lips onto mine. My peach cobbler bubbled, sending its sweet aroma into the air.

"I got a room for a few days if you want to get away." He spoke in between kisses as he worked his lips down my chest, burrowing his face into my shirt.

I almost didn't think we would make it to the room, but we did!

Unclothed, we intertwined. Donald touched every surface of me, internally and externally, exploring every hole in my body from my mouth to anal. His physique glistened as he towered over me, using a cloth to clean himself.

Licking his lips, giving me a cunning grin, the man dove in headfirst, eating my purring lady like she was the appetizer, main course, and dessert. The way this man devoured my vagina, I could've sworn he was being starved at home. Climaxing, I grabbed his head and attempted to push him away. He clutched my arms and pinned them to the bed, licking me until my soul exited my body.

Mary J's voice took me out of my thoughts as I turned the volume up, snapping my fingers and mouthing the words to the song.

"I can love you better than she can. Sitting here
Wondering why you don't love me
The way that I love you and baby have no fear
Cause I would never ever hurt you
And you know my love is real, boy, I can...."

I picked up my drink and danced my way into the kitchen, stirring the pot to our dinner. I looked down at my phone, and time had gotten away from me, and apparently away from Donald. It wasn't like him to be late. In fact, he was a stickler for timeliness.

Dialing his number, something inside of me didn't sit right. The phone rang once and went straight to voicemail.

"I know the hell he didn't!" I scoffed. It never disturbed me before; I knew he had a family, and he would not always be at my beck and call. But today, I felt rejected, abandoned, and some other weird emotions that have never surfaced before. As time went on, I saw him; differently I saw us in a different light. Maybe we, what if he, or what happens when our friendship blossoms. Will it blossom? Our feelings for each other were undeniable. We professed our love to one another, and I knew that we could never become what we wanted by remaining what we are.

I had decided! I would give him an ultimatum, and today, he would have to choose. I called him one more time, then another and another.

"Hello?"

I put my hand over my mouth as my mouth had gone dry, but I didn't dare swallow.

"Hello?" The voice sang, now a little more piercing than before. The unwarranted tears fell from my face

"So, you are going to just breathe in my ear? What's the matter? I wasn't the voice you were hoping to hear? I'm pretty sure he will be arriving shortly. He had other matters to tend to. Matters that don't and never would include the likes of you. Tell me, how does it feel? What is it like to know that it's still not your court even when you have the ball? The ball may travel back and forth, but it's left in the home team's court when the game ends. Let that marinate Miss Thing."

The phone call ended, and the locks on the door turned simultaneously. Donald walked through, just as dapper as ever. He held a bouquet of flowers in one hand and a Louise Vuitton bag in the other.

I put the phone to my chest as the tears flowed down my face. His facial expression read a look that I had never seen before—hearing the voice of his wife had made her more accurate than ever before.

Donald and I never spoke of her. He never complained, uplifted, or even crooned anything about her. I didn't even know her name, and to be honest, I didn't care to, yet it also made it appear as if she didn't exist. At least, that's what I wanted to believe.

"We need to talk." He spoke, sending me into a sickening spell instantly. As the words escaped from his mouth, I dropped to my knees; the world around me paused. The room temperature increased, and my eyes burned as the site of the Goddess herself punctured my soul.

Goddess Speaks!

"Get your emotional behind off the floor and face the repercussions before you! Lift thy head as I empty my wrath on you and splurge my fury against ye! Need I remind you of, **Get out of your feelings, 1:2** *Thy feelings of a side chick will never take precedence over the Queen that holdeth thy throne.*' Unfortunately, I have had to stop my evening meditation to reiterate the importance of not catching feelings in this game.

I don't have time to soothe you with lies and demise, my poor lost child. You allowed a wet tongue, a long, thick, well-used penis, and intertwining emotions. What should have remained a flirty friendship took you out of your element and into the pits of emotional hell.

How many times do I have to tell you that if you don't control the mind, the mind will control you? Apparently, you allowed your mind to take you on a wild goose chase of false hopes and unrealistic expectations.

You already were aware of the risks, and you took them anyway, knowing exactly where things would go if you fell too deep into your whack-ass emotions. As a result, you attempted to trade in a temporary situation merely led by misdirected feelings. Despite better judgment, you sustained forward, hoping that he will trade in his queen for, well, I'll just say it.

A fucking pawn!

I'm sorry, but I'm not sorry! I cannot help but judge you according to your ways and bring about your disgrace. The queen in you entered another queen's monarchy, creating demands that her king was in no position to make. What in the hell did you think was going to happen? You and he would go into the church singing, 'I choose you?' I think thee fuck not!

You are not *Erykah Badu*, and Donald is nowhere near *Andre*.

13

Burn in Hell Bitch!

DAILY READS!

Let me first say whenever you enter a situation as a pawn; it doesn't mean in any way, shape, or form that you cannot make it to the other side of the chessboard. The "pawn" is a mere "immature" and "hopeful" side chick. The more strategic a pawn is, the more powerful they become. However, they have no authority to make any demands or requests until the pawn is promoted. Though many pawns' fundamental goal is promotion, there is never a guarantee in *Side Chick Land*.

No matter how strategic, even when the pawn reaches the other side of the chessboard, it is still up to the player to choose what piece he wants to promote. The queen is one of the most influential pieces on the board; feelings hold no precedence over her position in her monarchy. She knows that feelings cloud judgment, and logic become illogical. The queen has the prerogative to appoint, dismiss, regulate, and declare war. Trust me; you don't want to go to war with a true queen.

You will lose every time!

But please understand, *Side Chick Paradise* can be a monarchy of its own. A true side chick is a queen in her own dominion. Here, she holds all the keys and creates her own boundaries and standards. It could all be so simple on this ground, yet one makes it hard by allowing the emotions and power to manipulate the mind. Whether one wants to admit it or not, she is a significant threat. Many have written her off as a desperate and thirsty imbecile that can't find her king, and so forth. But a true side chick that knows her place is nothing of such. In all actuality, she is a peril and will check your ass before you can even say, mate.

We have all seen *Scandal* and Tyler Perry's, *Sista's*, where side chicks prevail, and like it or not; it happens in the real world as well. A true side chick is a queen with more power than one gives her credit for. She doesn't catch feelings; she catches flights. She makes realistic demands of the king, and she requires reciprocity. She knows her value, maintains her cool, and is the logic and the sole reason behind the king's newfound peace. With that, the king will do whatever it takes to make and keep her happy. She is not a piece he is willing to lose.

Becoming a side chick is risky for everyone involved. However, as the side chick, it is your responsibility alone to keep your feelings in check; easier said than done, but you signed up for this, sis. Adding an additional love variable to the equation may result in increased complications and expectations that your partner simply did not ask for. There are many issues with getting attached; he might get turned off and cut you out completely. If you choose to defy this rule, you will have to prepare yourself for the repercussions that follow.

Remember, the immature side chick complains about the wind, the hopeful-side chick expects it to change, and the successful side chick adjusts the sails.

Which one are you?

Side chick affirmation of the day!

Say this aloud and repeat it!
"I catch flights, not feelings!"
Side chick-alations
2

LAW THREE
Thou Shall Always Use Protection

"When the woman felt his flesh was better and more pleasing to her insides. It was desirable for obtaining a more intense orgasm. She allowed him to entice her with sweet promises of tomorrow, permitting him to enter her unprotected. His sperm then intermingled with her eggs. Then the man said unto her, you must not keep the baby, for I will not leave my wife and kids."

The lies he tells 3: 1-4

Monica "The Risky Side Chick"
Mamas Baby, Daddy Played Me!

I sat on the terrace of the hotel and watched in bliss. The view alone was incredible. There was an unobstructed view of the ocean from the balcony, which was just breathtaking. We watched the sunset taking in Hawaii's lovely trade winds this morning as I made circles in his chest. I studied the Breaching Whales and Lounging Turtles in absolute delight. Marc had provided everything I needed, if not more, on this all-expense-paid trip to Maui. I deserved every bit of it if I didn't say so myself.

18

I keep an eye on him as he interacts with the children; even with his lower region wrapped in a beach towel, I could see the print of his manhood. He looked up in my direction, giving me a wink and a smile. I returned the gesture, bringing my cocktail to my lips.

Clara sifted her feet across the private white sandy beach. Her thick, blonde ponytail swayed side to side as she ambled over to him, gracing him with an intimate hug and long sensual kiss. You would think her actions would evoke some form of resentment or envy. Yet, it had done the contrary. It pleasured me, stimulating every sensual sensor deep within me.

Clara was gorgeous, fit, and appeared to be everything Marc loved in a woman. Yet something was missing, and that something was me. Dating a married man sent a rush of excitement through me. The fact that we could sneak around and no one knew about us made this more exhilarating. This trip took the cake. Marc could never go four days and three nights without me.

After our first night together, he sent me a charming message that read,

I started missing you before you even left this morning.

It went from that to,

We should start doing this more often. I'm considering leaving her.

I never fell for the false promises and never anticipated him to leave his high-school sweetheart. I enjoyed things as they were. There were many perks to this life; I was sure to take advantage of every one of them. After all, this isn't my first rodeo.

My phone buzzed, sending me on an exciting wave.

Marc: I need someone to kiss me right now. Come now!

I walked into my room and put on my maid outfit. Even though I had my own room, Marc got off on the thought of me joining him in his. So much that he made sure that our rooms were on the same floor, just down the hall. I smiled cunningly as I watched Clara and the kids make sand beach angels.

I gave the door a rat-a-tat before twisting the knob. "Room service." I sang, closing the door behind me. Marc emerged from behind the door, rushing me from behind. He picked me up and placed me on the granite countertop, lifting my skirt and spreading my legs wide.

"How long do we have?" I asked in between the panting.

"Not long." His fingers fasten around mine, solid and secure, like every part of him. I pulled my hand from his and grabbed his lower region, guiding it into mine. Snapping out of lust and into reality, I came to my senses.

"Wait!" I objected, ripping the condom wrapper open with my teeth.

"Come on, Monica, just this once, baby." He moaned while continuing to stroke me intensely, delving into my internal organs, spelling all kinds of obscenities with his range of motion.

Feeling his flesh inside of me made me cream more than ever before, but I knew better. I pushed him back and placed the condom on him. Giving me an intense glare, he rammed himself inside of me, pounding me in palpable frustration.

"You don't like the way I feel inside of you?" He grimaced, picking me up and throwing me across the bed.

"Don't you want me to feel every part of you?" He crooned, mounting me from behind. He placed his hand on the small of my back, creating an arch, bringing my ass upward.

I felt a spasm in the wake of my ribcage; for a moment, I felt something strange. I shook out of my thoughts, but the feeling that graced me was flesh, mixed with something else.

Was this emotion? It can't be. No, it's nothing, all just hormones and boredom and the attraction of the forbidden. I must make him put the condom back on.

I parted my mouth to speak. Marc gripped his free hand around my neck and stroked me passionately. I could feel a strong urge coming on as he stroked me harder.

Tell him he must stop, the voice in my head demanded. *This is not a good idea.*

But it feels so good. I thought. I couldn't stop him; instead, I threw my head back and pushed myself towards him, begging him to dive deeper.

"I love you, Monica." He professed in between breaths. "You will always belong to me." He continued.

A shiver runs through my body, and my blood starts to race. Feeling the warmth spread throughout me, Marc's penis throbbed inside me.

"We have to stop." I panted, still pushing myself against him.

Marc stroked fast and harder, causing me to climax uncontrollably.

"Oh, shit!"He panted, pummeling me more complex and more demanding, spilling his seeds into my garden.

"Fuck!" he spat, laying his head on my back.

It was at that moment I knew; I had just fucked up!

"Here are your results, my dear. And here is a brochure with all of your options." P.A, Burke, that's how she introduced herself, slid both across the desk toward me.

"Guessing by the date you gave; I am pretty sure your options are becoming slim."

My brows furrowed, but I remained silent as she indicated I might not be fit for this, and judging by my situation, she may be right.

"Thank you; it looks like I have some thinking to do. If that's all, I'll get back to work. I'm on break." I added, forcing a smile.

I reached for the papers as she searched my eyes for a hint of emotion. She places her hand on mine.

"I'm okay, trust me. My boyfriend is going to be stoked." I lied, patting her hand before removing mine.

I walked out of the doctor's office and dialed Marc's number. It has been three weeks and four days, and he hasn't even returned my calls. I put the phone to my ear.

"The number you have called is not in service."

Rattled, I brushed shoulders with a lady, not paying attention to where I was going.

"Excuse me." Just as the words left my mouth, I looked up, and there stood Clara and her protruding belly. A lump formed in my throat as Marc appeared behind.

My eyes filled with fury; I slapped the papers onto his chest and rushed away, not once turning back.

The words to *Julia Coles*, "Sidepiece," blared in my head…

That's what you call your side piece
White lie little stories
Tryna hide it from me
Bless her heart, that poor thing
Honey, I'm so sorry
It's too bad you gon' miss me
When you reach for the real thang
And all you feel is lonely
You can call your side piece oh
Go head call your side piece oh
A little lapse in judgment
A messed up nothing fling
A million I'm so sorrys
Swear she don't mean a thang
A moment of weakness
Just wasn't thinking straight
A ride down the wrong road
A stupid mistake,

22

Running out of the door, I slid into the pits of hell as The Goddess greeted me with her presence.

The Goddess

I shake my head in disbelief, blazing with fury and disappointment.

"Monica, you were always one of my favorite girls. You knew precisely what this life required and enjoyed every bit of it. No matter how many sweet lies Marc sang into your ear, you were wise enough to recognize the game and understand that Marc's unyielding love for Clara would surpass your position in his life.

So, I can't seem to understand for my life how in the hell you ended up dumb and filled with cum.

How often must I drill into your pretty little head that it doesn't matter what the man says to convince you; as a side piece, it is always your obligation to know your position and hold your ground.

For Pete's sake, the man has five kids! Two of which were outside of the marriage, might I add. I am sure he didn't tell you that shit." I scoffed in disgust.

The Lies he Tells, 3:1-4 *'When the woman felt his flesh was better and more pleasing to her insides. It was desirable for obtaining a more intense orgasm. She allowed him to entice her with sweet promises of tomorrow, permitting him to enter her unprotected. His sperm then intermingled with her eggs. Then the man said unto her, you must not keep the baby, for I will not leave my wife and kids.'*

Still, you decided to break the vow you made with your hand on the Side Chick law book! Allowing him to release his cock-eyed ass minions into your arid ass village.

I have drilled the importance of not allowing her man to feel you in the raw. There is no need to cry and become enraged at a man such as Marc doing precisely what he's expected to do. You let him to go skinny dipping in your ocean pissing in the water, leaving you singing a sad tune of Mama's Baby, Daddy Played Me! You are a risk-taker indeed, but no one told your goofy ass to jump off the plane without the parachute.

Congratulations, you played yourself!

Now you look like a damn spare tire thrown out on the side of the road. Clueless and useless. This one hurt a Sista, but the law is the law. You knew the rules of the game, yet you ignored them and broke the law.

To Side chick, hell you go," I demanded.

"Burn in hell!"

DAILY READ

on't shoot the messenger, but it is no surprise that side chicks have been around long before you readers existed and will be here long after you are gone. They are even in the bible. Don't believe me? Go to *Genesis chapter 16.* Though Abraham's wife Sarai's idea to include Hagar in the mix of their marriage, once Sarai became envious and supposed that Hagar's pregnancy would be the cause of despise, she ordered Abraham to deal with her. As a result, Hagar was sent away, and into the wilderness, she'd go.

Though Abraham had a child with Hagar, it did not place Hagar on a par with Sarai. Hagar and her son were left to settle in the wilderness, and even when Abraham disagreed, Abraham was ordered by God himself to respect his wife's decision to send the mother of his child and his away.

I can't express enough how you must protect yourself and everything that comes with you in this game. Your peace of mind, emotional well-being, and your physical well-being. One night of passion can become a lifetime of pain. In the story, Monica allowed temporary passion to redirect her standards, throw off her balance, and fall into the pit of burning desire.

A side piece's sole purpose is for her pleasure; her wants, needs, and desires, minus the extra baggage of many relationships. You stay in your lane and don't create any traffic. Here, you get great sex, some cuddling from time to time, gifts, new tits, butt lifts, and whatever else you yearn for. The best part of it all is you don't have to deal with his trifling ass outside of that. He is her problem, not yours.

I read from an article in Medical Daily, where relationship expert Chris Armstrong. He stated, *"If someone is tired of the dating scene and is strictly looking for a physical piece of the pie, being the other person is not going to offend them because they are not looking for anything more serious."*

Being a side chick is like working a seasonal position between jobs or summer breaks. You create the way you want to treat this position. Just know it's temporary work that encourages a good work ethic and incentives. They are not meant to be forever. They may decide that you are no longer needed, but if they like you and it is in their budget, they will surely keep you around. You can determine if you want to stick around or find a position that fits your requirements and transition to something more secure and long-term.

First, who's to say he is only sleeping with you and her; who is to say his woman doesn't have a little piece on the side herself? You are already sharing a man; now, you are transferring bodily fluids and bacteria and putting yourself at risk of things that some may view as far more troubling than a child. You should never think twice about taking control of your sexual health and safety. Always stay ready, remain on your toes, and be wise, no matter what he says.

Many of these men are just lost little squirrels chasing a nut, and that nut can come from any and everywhere. Therefore, you make the rules and gauge how the relationship goes. You protect yourself at all costs. And you don't let up, no matter what he tells you. Besides, the lies he tells and the secrets he keeps are why you are on this side of the coin in the first place.

Side chick affirmation of the day!
Say this aloud and repeat it!

"I will protect myself at all costs!"
Side chick-alations
3

LAW FOUR

Thou Shall Not Putteth Their Life on Hold

"Thy sat in the wasteland waiting patiently for him to join her, but he never came. For what he had built was far sturdier than the tempting floorplan that lacked foundation."

A House is Not a Home 4:1-3

Tammy "The Committed Side Chick."

No matter what you do, God can't save you!

he car rocked from side to side as the strong winds slapped the raindrops against the windows. The moans and panting were drowned out by the sweet sound of the *Atlantic Stars*, "Secret Lovers."

"Secret lovers, yea. That's what we are; we try so hard to fight the way we feel. We both belong to someone else, and I can't let go; what we feel is oh so real...."

Barry crooned the lyrics in my ear while nibbling my lobe in between adlibs. Every time his lips touched any part of my body, I shivered from head to toe.

Barry and I met as teens. After being sent to live with my Nana when my brother Charlie was murdered, he was one of my first friends. His father, the small-town church home pastor, delegated Barry to make me feel like family and look after me. I loved Barry from the moment I laid eyes on him, but he never knew until one of the girls in the church stole my diary and spilled all my tea in front of the entire youth group. That was the day my quiet, reserved tail came out of the shell. Putting a southern ass-whooping on a big-mouth girl named Myesha from Detroit. The next day, I was off to college and only seen Barry in between breaks, never speaking of the confessions in my diary.

After finishing school and going through a terrible break-up, I came back to find my Nana ill and in total debt. I took on the role of the choir director, and Barry was the new Deacon of the church. He invited me over one evening for a movie like old times and to catch up. Dead smack in the middle of the movie; I kissed his lips, and the film ended up watching us.

Barry was the first and only guy I had ever given myself to, and I had replayed that scene in my head so many times before that one. I just never expected it to end with a phone call from a fiancé he forgot to mention in the midst of our "catching up."

But none of that mattered to me; I loved Barry and believed that once he saw that I was the woman he was meant to be with, he would never marry Ericka. I gave Barry loyalty and wanted him to know that I came back before he made the worst decision of his life and married the wrong woman.

Six months later, we are still having sex in the back of my little ass car, seizing the moments, and sleeping the nights away into early mornings. In these moments, Barry is filled with uncertainties and second-guesses up until he busses a nut, falls asleep, and gets a sudden burst of repentance in the morning.

Then it's back to the regular, "I'm just not sure how you expect this to work, Tammy. We are in this car and not out in the streets because of the heat we would get if anyone gets wind of you and me. We are both very upstanding members of the church, and you already know that being the son of the preacher man comes with a whole other expectation." He kissed me on my forehead and buttoned up his shirt.

"I get it, Barry, I do, but…" his phone ringing interrupted my speech. Barry put his finger over his mouth, quieting me before placing the call on speaker.

"Good morning, my handsome King." Ericka sang.

I squirmed in my seat when I heard her voice.

"Hey, my beautiful Queen." Barry chimed as a broad grin spread across his face.

"Have you talked to your friend Tammy lately?" She asked, catching us both off guard.

This was it; we have been found out. I thought, placing my hand over my mouth. I was filled with a sense of relief.

"What makes you ask?" Barry stutters.

Yes, we have been sleeping together, and yes, we love one another, let it go! The firm voice in my head had spoken.

"Well, I saw Bianca from one of my old charity groups at the nail salon. She told me Tammy had planned her wedding, and the pictures were immaculate. Now, I have never been a fan of her singing and have always thought she could use some vocal lessons; but her wedding planning skills are on point!"

I was torn in between the "*Oh no, she didn't*" and the Cardi lip pop with a snap.

"Yea, I heard she's pretty good at what she does." Barry smiled cunningly.

I rolled my eyes and shook my head in agitation.

"You think she will plan our wedding?"

I almost choked in between hyperventilating. Barry sent me a barely concealed look telling me to pull it together.

Hesitating, Barry's eyes searched my face for reluctance. "I'm sure she would be delighted." He lied, giving my thigh a warm squeeze.

Then it's decided!" Ericka perked. "I will talk to her today at church and hire her as our Wedding Planner."

———— ❦ ————

"Girl, what did you say?"

"I didn't even know what to say, Dez! I don't know what to do or say." I cradled the phone between my ear grabbed bottled water out of the fridge. Feeling stiffness in my back, I took a long stretch. "I do know one thing; I am tired of us humping in the back seat of my car. If we do this any longer, I swear my chiropractor bill will shoot through the roof."

"And we both know you can afford that." Dez spat.

"I can't be mad at you on that one; I definitely can't afford another bill. Which is why I am going to say yes." I sighed.

"Tammy, no! You are treading thin, sis. This will not end well for you and.."

"Tam!" My grandmother called from her room.

"I gotta go, Dez."

I walked back to my grandmother's room, and she was sitting up stiff as can be holding her bible in her lap. "Have a seat, baby." Her sweet voice crooned as she tapped the spot next to her.

I sat next to Nana and ran her fingers through my auburn coils. "I always loved your curls, baby." She hummed.

"Awe, thanks, Nana, you always gave me such inspiration when the kids on the block would tease me and call me Curly locs." I chuckled.

"Ole nappy head chirren." Nana scoffed in between what seemed to be a painful cough.

"You need some water?"

"No, baby, I'm okay. Tell me something, why don't I see you go out with any of these handsome fellas around here?"

"Oh Nana, I don't have the time or energy to date; with choir rehearsal and planning weddings, I can't find the time." I waved dismissively.

"You sure? Because I'd like to think that Barry would have

something to do with that."

My heart rate increased; I was taken entirely off guard. But Nana always had a way of knowing. The only one who knew about Barry and me was my friend Dez, and she lives across the country.

"That man doesn't deserve you, or any woman for that matter. He is entitled and inconsiderate to the women in his life. No one wins here, chile. And you are putting your life on hold for a man that..."

"That I have loved since I was fourteen, Nana! It just; just feels like he and I were divine, meant to be, and God.."

"Ah-ah..don't do that."

"Do what?" I sighed in frustration.

"Don't bring God into this mess. He ain't got nothing to do with you and Barry's choices; people got that bad. Yall do what you will but don't start bringing God into the equation to justify your poor choices."

"Who says my choices are poor, huh? Who says I'm not doing what I feel is right for me? Why can't I fight for what I and who I want? I have lost everyone I loved, and you and Barry are all I have left. My mother sent me away because she didn't know how to love me properly. My father never even acknowledged me, and now the man that I love is staying in a relationship he doesn't even want because of what the "church" community would say about him." My heart rate began to increase as the tears poured from my eyes.

"I will not give up, I am staying here by his side, and I don't care how long it takes." I protested.

My grandmother's eyes saddened, "your father didn't acknowledge you because he had his own family, and your mother assumed that because his wife was unable to give him children, having you would make him love her more. She, too, was set on waiting for something or someone that never came. She never dated anyone and allowed herself to wither away like an unwatered rose.

Unfortunately, she did not bring you into the world because she wanted you, and she didn't send you away to protect you. Once she learned that your father and his wife adopted, she could no longer stand the sight of the poor choices she had made over someone that would move forward with their life, even when she put hers on hold."

My grandmother laid back in her bed and pulled the covers up to her chest.

Grammy knawed her gums and shook her head from side to side, "you made this bed, but it's up to you to decide how long you will stay here." She yawed.

"No matter what you do, God can't save you. Leave God out of this mess. You have to save ya self chile." She asserted before closing her eyes and going back to sleep.

I stood at the back of the church, patting my eyes with a tissue. Barry had really gone through with it, and I had planned the entire thing. This was supposed to be my wedding, not Ericka's. After Barry and Ericka had said their vows and his father pronounced them husband and wife, my shoulders dropped in defeat as I turned to exit the building.

"No, wait, Tammy," Ericka called out as I made it into the foyer.

Stopping in my tracks, I wiped my face hurriedly so she wouldn't see me cry.

Turning to face her, I forced a smile. "Congratulations!"

She grabbed my hand and smiled back, "This was so beautiful, honey; I mean, you did this as if it were your own!" Her condescending tone caught me off guard.

Clearing my throat, I pleasantly replied. "I'm glad you liked it."

She pulled me in for a hugged and whispered into my ear. "I knew about you the whole time, sweetie; I just wanted you to see what you could never have. I wanted you to know that you were nothing more than an empty little house, and I was his home." She snickered.

I broke away from her hold and gave her a sinister glare. We locked eyes, and she pursed her lips together, saying, "A house is made of barriers and woods that leave you with unpleasant splinters and spleens; a home is constructed with affection and unions crowned with love and dreams.

There's nothing half pleasant in coming home again. Here! Home! It is where love dwells. Beautiful memories are etched and stitched, family and friends unite as we bask in neverending laughter. Go back to your empty ass house; you are not welcome in our home!" She scoffed.

I snatched away from her wanting to sock the hell out of her right then and there. My nostrils flared, and my game face had left.

"There she is!" Barry perked, emerging from the sanctuary. Both of our eyes widened as we smiled in unison.

He walked over, grabbed his wife by the small of her back, and kissed her ever so sweetly. A lump was shaped in my throat, forcing me to swallow.

"The guests are waiting, and I am starving." He grabbed Ericka by the hand and pulled her away, never once acknowledging me.

Ericka shot me a look over her shoulders, "Well, let's get my husband fed; we know no one likes a side dish served cold." She snickered, giving me a wink and a smile.

Darting out of the church, I lost my balance and tumbled down the church stairwell; I dropped down, stopping at a set of Christian Louboutin Red bottoms. I looked up, only to find a menacing glare staring down at me.

The Goddess

I reached down and pulled Tammy up to face me. "Walk with me, child," I ordered, leading her into the reception hall.

We stood and watched as the chatter filled the room; the giggles and composition synced perfectly.

"Do you see anyone looking for you? Don't answer that; no one is looking for you. They don't even seem to notice that you are gone. You put your heart and soul into decorating this place, and the only thing in the room that matters at this moment is the bride and the groom. Barry continues with his life, his plans, none of which ever really included you.

You made excuses for him, you justified his behavior, and you placed your life on pause only to assist him in moving forward with his. Your love came with a sacrifice that was not at all reciprocated. You allowed delusion to dilute your disposition and gave him all of what he gave to her.

A House is Not a Home 1:2-3, *'Thy sat in the wasteland waiting patiently for him to join her, but he never came. For what he had built was far sturdier than the tempting floorplan that lacked foundation.'*

You put the building of your house on hold in hopes that he would come to a house that lacked structure, solidity, and value. You turned down gifts and money and chose to struggle; you put all your goals aside and pushed him to follow through with his. You made everything easy and didn't require him to merit anything from you. You even turned down a job that came with more benefits to remain close to a man that didn't even have the decency to get you a hotel room with a comfy mattress to fuck you. Now ya back is all jacked up, and you cant even ask him to pay for a chiropractor or can afford it ya self for that matter.

Not one time did he ever thank you for your kind efforts or even stop to see that you were, in fact, the woman that was willing to do whatever it took to bring him happiness and peace. You remained a sitting duck and put yourself in a position to be attacked and left for dead for a stiff dick clown that came with a lazy ass two-minute, my bad 60 second fuck.

There you were, fighting for this position, and you won absolutely nothing.

Congratulations!

I told you if you are going to live this life. Keep the expectations and false hopes out of it. Enjoy the ride for what it is. He never had any intention to keep you around, and there were three other church members Barry strung along too. Men like Barry are hunters; they get you, play with you, and when he gets tired of you, he will throw you away. To him, you were just another girl willing to take the bare minimum.

Wake up my sister and break the curse. You could have done far better than that fool. He ain't even know how to wipe his ass correctly; what did you expect? This whole damn dynamic was funky. Yet and still, you broke the rule. You put your life on pause for a man with shitty drawls.

Burn in Hell!

DAILY READ

he side chick's position is by choice, not by force, often in place because many don't want full-time partners. They want the thrill without the baggage. The connection without the attachment and the perks without the contract. They have other things that are far more enjoyable than doing the laundry, baking, cleaning, or going all through the day-to-day mill with him. They make the most of it minus the extra tasks and add-ons.

A loyal and committed side chick comes with a different level of side chick-ology. She somehow got a separate memo and truly loves the man that isn't hers. Her mind is set, and she has no plans to leave him unless, of course, he breaks her heart, and even that is a gamble. She is one of the most dangerous specimens because she doesn't give up, and for her, a glimmer of hope is all she needs.

Everyone wants to be loved; a man who receives love from a woman who openly knows he is not hers and is still willing to shower him with love and loyalty thickens the plot. She is good for his ego. An egotistical man can never be suitable for any woman on either side.

The advantage of sustaining a relationship of any sort with a side chick is to 'have his cake and eat it too.' He doesn't believe he will get caught, and most times, he doesn't care if he does. His ego serves him the notion that neither woman will leave, or he disposes of them when they no longer appease his appetite. Yet they want to be the only cuisine on your dish.

If you sign up for or choose to play this role, It is never your "the side chicks" job to convince another woman's man that he loves you.

It is not your job to wave this magic wand in his face to make him see that you are the magic potion to his happily ever after. The "why her and not me?" questionnaires don't come with fillable bubbles of newfound symphonies and epiphanies. It all boils down to understanding who and what you are dealing with.

Before you commit yourself to a person already in a committed relationship, please note that they have not left their significant other for a reason. There could be many reasons, such as not wanting to complicate or destroy the life they have built with their partner. Or as simple as they are with the one they want a future with and you are there for an enjoyable and peaceful time; in other words, you are the vacation day in the middle of a hard work week.

If you want to be in a relationship, contemplate moving on to someone who isn't already occupied in one and who wants a relationship with you too. Let's face it, many of these men create shit they cannot or will not clean up. The whole situation ends with bullshit that doesn't smell sweet and another sad love song left on repeat.

Cancel that flight and take another trip!

Side chick affirmation of the day!
Say this aloud and repeat it!

"I will not put my life on pause for a man with shitty drawls."
Side chick-alations
4

LAW FIVE

Thou Shall Not Kiss and Tell

"Be not careless with your mouth, for thy mouth can write you a check; thy behind cannot cash."

Remain discreet 5:1

Jade "The Attention Seeking Side Chick"

What you seek, you will find

"I'm just saying Jade, Sasha knew darn well what she was doing. Oh, and I didn't even tell you what Mike told me. He said…."

"Girl, I am not trying to be on this phone gossiping with you all day. I just called to ask you if you wanted to go to the *All-White* Party next week with me. That's it!?" I sucked my teeth in agitation, rolling my eyes.

Gabby let out a reluctant, "I guess." Under her breath. Gabby was too damn gossipy for me.

"I wasn't trying to be rude, Gabby. Sometimes, I get tired of hearing about everyone else and their drama, shits draining. Then, I am left to carry that toxicity with me for the rest of the day. It is hard as hell to shake it off." I patted my head and took a deep breath.

"I already have plans...."

"Cancel them! It's a day party!"

I'm sure it is! You know you need to get to ya boo in time."

"I ain't got no boo...." I interjected, smacking my lips.

"You know what? I'm not doing this with you. You act like you don't post side views of this man while he sleeps and add photos on social media with that big dumb ass emoji covering the man's face. But okay, I digress." Gabby chuckled.

I twisted my face and scrunched up my nose; Gabby was on point, though, but she had a big ass mouth, and once you let her get a sip of tea, she spilled the whole kettle. For four years now, Kareem and I have been doing this, whatever this may be. He and his girl Brandi have been on and off, off, and on for six years. Three kids, four if you are counting my ten-month-old baby Keenan.

All my family and friends think baby Keenan's daddy was killed in a bad car accident. And no, I did not sleep with him unprotected, the condom broke, and I was on the pill. Why did I keep the baby, you ask? I found out I was pregnant the day I went into labor; long story. Trust and believe had I known I was pregnant; there would have been no question where I would've gone. Needless to say, my prince is here, and I wouldn't trade him for anything; but he definitely threw a wrench in my plans.

Kareem started as a trick, Nah not that kind of trick, I'm nobody's hoe! He started out coming up to my job, flashing money and fast-talking. I have never liked those types of dudes. The kind of guys who think money can buy love and a sack earns them a quick nut. After being through multiple heartbreaks and unnecessary heartaches, I had decided all men were to be written off. If I gave them any play, I would never take them seriously!

Once he realized that his money wasn't going to shift the beat of my drum, he let his guard down and became his true self. He was super goofy and mad funny; there wasn't a day that he wouldn't make me laugh, and he always kept a smile on my face.

Kareem grew on me; he wasn't no ugly dude, so that wasn't the issue; ya boy was beyond the fine, okay. Chocolate skin, full, clean beard that hung down to his chest. Tall, deep dimples, and a fitness junkie.

Kareem and I were just cool; we would roll up, play video games, and talk shit until the sun came up. Brandi constantly accused him of doing something, and she wanted to remain clueless about how much he really loved her. She kicked him out every other night and flipped when he found his own spot. I knew he wasn't lying about her uppity ass because he would sometimes mute the phone and let me hear how toxic her slow ass was. We would put the phone on mute and laugh at her goofy ass.

She didn't have a clue what she wanted from the man, and if anything, she should have thanked me because, in the beginning, I was giving him tips and tricks to do, but her ass was never satisfied. He really didn't want to cheat on her, and all he really wanted was for someone to talk nice to him and call him a king every now and again. Shit, after all the crap I had been through, he was a breath of fresh air; I just closed the window whenever I felt a breeze.

I let Kareem spend his money and care for me, and I still didn't let him hit. The hell do I look like screwing somebody else's man? Sometimes he would come through, sit in between my legs, and let me play in his hair; Beautiful long, thick ass hair, might I add. Of course, I fed him. Hell, he was already in between my thighs, and it seemed like he was always starving, and I had no issue providing Kareem all of the nutrition he required, but that's as far as we went. On top of that, I showed him how to get in touch with his higher self. He needed it because Brandi was a low vibrational ass bitch.

Kareem paid every bill here, and after two and a half years of getting no twat, it was the least I could do. One night, He and Brandi were at odds, which was becoming the norm, and he asked if he could crash at my spot. I threw him a pillow and blanket and took my ass straight back to bed, I had to be at work early, and I didn't have time to be up all-night belly laughing with this man.

I lay in my bed, restless as I was graced with a sudden throb in my lower region. I hadn't felt a man inside of me in so long; I was sure there were all sorts of cobwebs in my coochie. I tossed and turned, put the pillow in between my legs, and held them together so tight I thought I'd seen cotton fluff floating in the air.

Suddenly, I felt a warm body and a hard dick on my back. Kareem took his hand and grabbed my hair before I could tell him to get his naked black ass out of my bed.

"Don't say shit." He whispered in my ear. Gripping my hair, bringing my head back towards him.

Kareem stuck his thumb inside of me, placing it on my hood, and rubbed gently. Pulling me into his stomach, I could hear him putting on the condom, and I didn't even stop him; in fact, he was taking too damn long if you asked me. I gasped as he entered my pool and went for a swim. I swear, the girth of this man filled my insides, sending me in overflow. My muscles tightened with every stroke, gripping him so tight he damned near suffocated. Yall, I swear, my mouth had a mind of its own and clamped shut, all while my river opened wide and streamed wetness down my legs.

I tried to maintain my rhythm to his flow as he wrote a whole damn cursive sentence in my notebook. I could've sworn the sentence read, I love you, but when he started making zigzag motions and writing all these X's and O's, I forgot how to read between the lines. I could feel him getting ready to bust a rhyme, and I was delighted to become a feature. In between pants and moans, we both pushed harder, climaxing so hard we shook the whole room.

If that wasn't enough, this fool removed himself and pulled me in for a remix. This man rubbed his nose in it; the chin even got involved, and so did his fingers. He kissed my thighs, bit my ass, pushed back my legs, sucked my girl's lips, and ate my pie as his life depended on it.

My legs began to shake, and I started to scream so loud he stuck my panties in my mouth. Unable to contain me, my erectile tissue swelled; I relaxed my muscles, let go, and squirted all over this man's pretty little face. That was the night I decided Brandi's ungrateful ass was just gonna have to share.

Keeping things low-key was never an issue for me because he always made me feel like I was the only girl in the world. But every time we talked about how long he expected to keep us under wraps, he fussed about her using the kids as pawns. Brandi, who?

"And what about baby Keenan? He doesn't deserve to have a father?"

"Now you know that ain't fair, Jade. I do everything for my son."

"Everything but acknowledges him outside of these four walls, Kareem. Your mother died not even being able to meet him. He is your first and only son, and no one on your end even knows you have him. I don't give you any drama, and you want to keep me a secret. Me? But Brandi is a full-fledge Bi…." Before I could finish my rant, I went flying over the couch. Holding my face, I gave Kareem the deadliest scowl he'd ever seen coming from me.

"Don't you for one second think you are going to disrespect my woman and the mother of my three daughters!" He hissed.

My grimace turned to sadness as tears rolled down my face. Kareem walked towards me to comfort me, but I ran away and locked myself inside the bathroom.

"Jade! I am so sorry. I don't even know what came over me. I love you, and I love my son. If Brandi finds out, you already know she will take my daughters away from me. You don't understand; she has taken them out of state over assumptions. Just…."

Kareem grew silent, and as I got up to open the door, the sound of my front door slammed, followed by his engine revving up.

It's been two weeks since I heard from Kareem, and I'll be damned if I called him first. He sent money for the baby and still sent me money for this month's rent and my car payment but….

"Jade!" Gabby screamed, taking me out of my thoughts.

"What, bitch?" I snapped in annoyance.

"Do you hear me talking? I was asking what you were…."

Gabby had gotten quiet; my eyes shifted as I waited for her to finish talking.

"Awe, that is so sweet!" she squealed.

"What?" You smelling yo self again, huh?"

"No bitch, I'm smelling relationship goals." She chuckled.

"Here you go!"

"Girl, I am so serious; I'm tired of holding on to my pillow at night. Kareem and Brandi just got engaged, and these pictures are so beautiful."

My heart stopped, and I began to hyperventilate. The sound of his name sent a wave of shock through my body. I tried to pull myself together, putting the phone on speaker. My hands trembled as I scrolled through the pictures posted on Brandi's page.

"Awe, I didn't even know she was pregnant again!" Gabby squealed, making me angry. The information was coming quicker than I could process.

"And it's a boy! Their first boy at that! This is beyond cute, and she is working that dress. She doesn't even look… you know what? It's everything for me."

"Why in the hell do you let social media dictate your goals? You don't have a clue what those people got going on behind closed doors. Bitches kill me." I chuckled mockingly.

"Whoa, whoa! Where's this coming from? What happened to the 'oh-so-positive' bitch that I was talking to a minute ago? Go get her, please and thank you; because you got some nerve trying to dim my light of hopefulness! If I want a relationship like Brandi and Kareem, then let me live bitch!" Gabby snapped.

I sighed, inhaling deeply, pouring myself a glass of Ciroc. I tossed the cup back and let the burning sensation subside. My game face, my calmness, all of that had shifted, and my petty bitch had been activated.

"Listen, Gabby, all I'm saying is this, these bitches will post anything to put a façade on for the world. Brandi is a nut, and Kareem probably only stays with her because of their kids. And who's to say, that's his first son?" The words slipped out of my mouth, and there was an eerie silence.

"What do you know, Jade? You over there saying it with ya chest and shit. This ain't no hypothetical ass conversation, and I know when a bitch is in her feelings. I know damn well you ain't got the tea, or do you? Spill that shit!"

"Nothing to spill…." My tone calmed; I swallowed another shot. The emotion I felt had been suppressed deep inside me for the past year. Rage filled me as I stared at the picture of Kareem kissing Brandi's belly. Their daughters surrounded them on the rolled-out carpet as they sat Indian style; their dresses spread out, and their tiaras sparkled.

I couldn't understand what Kareem saw in a woman that didn't respect him as a man. A woman that would use her children to torture and mind fuck him. I had told him about his rights even found a lawyer that would help him attain joint custody, but his head was so far up Brandi's ass that he couldn't even see how much she would make his life a living hell and turn his world upside down whenever she damned well pleased.

Bitches like Brandi needed realities checks, and today, I would give her a whole damn epiphany! No longer will I linger in the darkness while she gets to savor the light. Today it was my time to shine; it was time to step out of secrecy and grace the stage with my presence and what a dramatic entrance it would be. I scrolled through my phone and found what I was looking for.

Gabby continued to blabber on and on as I sucked my teeth and allowed the sound of the drumroll to entice me. I pressed the button, and it was done. A picture of Kareem and baby Keenan dressed alike three weeks ago with a caption that read, *you forgot your prince, Kareem*, floated its way into the comment section of their big announcement. This muthafucka right here was grand.

Gabby gasped in disbelief; I could imagine the jaw-dropping expression on her face.

"That's what I thought." I hissed before clicking over.

"What the hell, Jade?!" I could hear Kareem panting out of breath in distress.

"Oh, did I ruin your little celebration?" I laughed mischievously.

"Dammit, Jade, I'm the last person you should be worried about! Where is my son?" He panicked.

"With my mom, they won't be back in town till tomorrow, and no, you can't sleep here! You fucking proposed to that bitch and had …."

"Jade, you need to get out of that house now! I told you Brandi ain't wrapped too tight; she is."

"What, Kareem? She ain't no crazier than the next; you think she the only one missing a few? You are the only fool scared of that lunatic.

46

She got your head so far in the clouds that you can't even be happy with the person that knows who you really are. She has no clue who you really are..."

"But she has a clue who the fuck you are! You just wrote a check; your ass can't cash! I'm out of this shit Jade. She ain't gone leave me, don't you get that shit?"

I paced the floor in indignation as I had tuned Kareem out; my heartbeat increased as I was flooded with comments, gifs, and memes under what I had posted. My fingers couldn't type quickly enough, and the words were coming in so fast my head was spinning. *The slurs and the threats were weaving together as they mocked my son and called me a delusional wanna-be-relevant ass side chick. What had I just done? Was this all worth it?*

"I ain't nobodies desperate ass whore; her man chased me around for years!" I screamed at the phone as if the people could hear me. Tears poured out my eyes, blurring my vision. I grabbed the whole bottle of Ciroc and took what was left straight to the face. The shit that people would say to make you look like you are the bad guy. Like I took Kareem hostage, stole his nut, and impregnated my damn self. Hell, I ain't even invite him to my place; she sent his ass here with her bipolar ass tantrums and insecure antics.

My phone kept ringing with private and blocked calls. Brandi and her lapdogs tagged me in posts made ads with my picture address and phone number. All of this in a matter of hours. I couldn't delete the comment if I wanted to; it had been screenshotted and used as a meme so much it had gone viral by the end of the night.

I buried my head in my face and tried to contemplate my way out of this. At this moment, I just wanted to be held and talked off the ledge. I was so over this whole damn situation. My phone sang "Little Secret" by *Xscape*, sending a rush of emotions through my body. That was Kareem's text notification.

You're my little secret; that's how we should keep it...

"Why didn't I just let it go?" I sobbed. I knew better than this shit. "Fucking pride, I tell you!" I threw my hands up and shook my head.

The ringing of my doorbell startled me. I took a deep breath and walked toward the door. My phone continued to play the song; I just ignored it, making a mental note to put my phone on silent for the rest of the night. I peered out the window, and no one was standing there. I'd be damned if I opened the door and took a peek, not today! Feeling unexpectedly intoxicated, I turned around and stumbled my way towards the sofa.

"It was not this damn hard walking to the door," I mumbled, grabbing hold of the wall. The rest of the distance from the door to the sofa appeared huge. Just as I reached the couch, I felt a blow to my head, sending me slumped over the arm of the furniture and into the darkness.

he pounding in my head was excruciating as I strained to open my eyes. My mouth was in agonizing pain as well, and as I went to rub my fingers across my lips, my hands were bound. My eyes widened at the sight of Brandi standing in front of me, pacing back and forth, mumbling under her breath.

I prepared to speak, but my mouth wouldn't open. I looked over to the mirror to my right, and my mouth had been sewn shut. Mortified, I closed my eyes and pretended to be still passed out. I had no clue what Brandi was going to do next, and I had to think my way out of this shit.

"Why these bitches, keep playing with me is beyond me. Why must they keep testing my limits? Kareem knew better; I warned him! Why do these men think they can keep embarrassing me? Why don't they know how to keep their whores' mouths shut?" She continued pacing back and forth, waving a shiny object in the air.

Between her rants and the pain I was feeling, I could barely think. I took a deep breath and thought back to my girl scout days and how to break free from a knot tie. I wiggled slowly as Brandi murmured threats tapping her head with the shiny object. Turning around swiftly, she had caught me with my eyes open.

"Oh, you are awake from your nap? Huh? I can't hear you!" She mocked, cupping her ear with her free hand.

I continued to wiggle my way out of the tie slowly without her noticing.

"See, I already knew about your weird-ass. I figured you knew to stay in your lane and remain lowkey. But noooooooo! You want to make a public announcement and get out ya body. I never even told Kareem I knew about you because of all the clowns I dated; Kareem has been by far the best. I just... I just don't know how to be peaceful. I need to know he loves me and the only love I am used to feeling is pain. I know, I know it's weird and..." Brandi sat down on the edge of my bed and dropped her head.

"I had a daddy, you know. He loved me very much." She nodded her head up and down; her demeanor was of a three-year-old girl.

I nodded with her, remaining calm as I was almost free from her tie.

"And my dad, he had to *show* me how much *he* loved me. He showed me love in ways I didn't know love could be shown." Brandi's voice softened, and she rocked back and forth, rubbing her thigh with her left hand and holding what I see now was a gun to her chest.

"He always told me, you never kiss and tell. You always keep your mouth closed and people out of your business!" Her voice raised as she shot up and grimaced in my direction.

"I had become addicted to physical pain. Not the pain that included a bandaid. The pain that my dad gave me, the beatings, the name-calling, the breaking boundaries, and when Kareem didn't do any of that, I started having withdrawals badly because pain to me is an addiction. It's like a drug addiction." She licked her lips and raised her brow.

Wandering away from me and towards my bedroom window, she continued. "Kareem is a different kind of man with a different kind of tolerance. I pushed and pushed, and he still never gave up on me until

49

you came around! I could tell when you came into the picture because he was not the same. He was less tolerant, more resilient, and...."

"No longer your punching bag!" I murmured, going upside her head with a vase.

Brandi stumbled, but the bitch didn't fall. She turned towards me as we wrestled back and forth. I tried to pry the gun from her; this heifer was strong as hell. Falling back over an object, Brandi fell on top of me, and the sound of the weapon punctured my ears.

The Goddess

I watched in disbelief as this whole thing unfolded before me. This all could have been avoided. Brandi's body fell limp onto Jades as she groaned in agony. Jade pushed her body over, freeing herself from underneath. The tears filled Brandi's eyes as Jade grabbed her phone from her pocket. She placed her hand on Brandi's wound with as much pressure as she could. Brandi coughed as blood seeped from the side of her mouth. It was already too late. She was gone. She was gone long before this, but that's another story for another time.

"Didn't I tell yo dumb coleslaw ass to stay out the light and remain in the shadows? Didn't I convey that you are nothing more than the French fries to his combo? Don't even think for a second that I didn't see the antics you've put on overtime. Yo, high-yellow ass has been trying to "expose" Kareem and your situation on the low for the past month. Posting subliminals, side shots, and all that other unnecessary madness.

This was no moment of weakness; you were waiting for the right opportunity to make an entrance and fell straight on your damn face. Now look at you, sitten there with ya mouth sewn shut; speechless. Can't even call for help. Regardless of how this went down, you signed that contract long before baby Keenan was born. You knew that Brandi was not going to let Kareem go without a fight, and this was a fight that was far past your weight class sista girl." I scoffed.

"You allowed your emotions and outside perceptions to lead you on a goose chase sending you on one way trip to overlapping disasters in which exposed a harsh reality; you were a non-factor! When you signed that contract, you knew damn well how this shit was gone play out. You knew that silence was golden, and even if his glitter wasn't gold, it was not your job to hold that up to the light.

Remain Discreet 5 vs 1, *'Be not careless with your mouth, for thy mouth can write ye a check, thy behind cannot cash.'* In other words, you have the right to remain silent; anything you say and do will be held against you and send your ass straight to the pits of side chick hell.

Burn in Hell!

DAILY READ!

L et's just face it! It's not easy being a side chick. There is a considerable risk of getting caught as a side chick, and sometimes it's inevitable. This is why privacy is paramount, and neglecting to adhere to this rule carries a higher risk of getting caught dead smack in the middle of a melodrama filled with schemes and scandals that Tyler Perry can't even write.

There is more to it than the bump and grind, gifts and trips, and the exhilaration it may give off. When you decide to play this role, you must master the art of being non-existent. You must learn how to remain in the shadows and reinvent yourself as Houdini; "Poof-be-gone," in a blink of an eye.

You do not exist! Remember?

Being the other woman requires you always to remain secretive and discreet. This is not the time to be braggadocios and all telling. This life comes with fake names and timelines lined with airtight mysteries spicier than Crime Time. There is no place for Blue's Clues here, leaving clues that will lead to unwanted trouble and never-ending feuds.

When the urge to be relevant is present, there is no telling what one is capable of. It can range anywhere from striking up random conversations that are littered with hints to posting pictures online of the side of his face with the cliché captions that read, "no face, no case." Either way, it's cheesy and classless.

TEN LAWS OF A SIDE CHICK

If you are a woman that likes to be shown off as someone's prize or trophy, this role is not for you! The suit doesn't fit hunty, and that is ok. But what is not ok is you making a grand entrance or performing a big reveal party because you are butt hurt or have decided somewhere along the line you want to be the main course in his meal.

This role is to your benefit; you create the storyline; however, that doesn't include inserting yourself into someone else's starring role when you are only an extra. Here, your options are always open. You are not in a relationship, and you are free to move with ease as you please. You answer no one, and woman-to-woman conversations don't fit your description and are not on this script. There is no room for adlibs and reenactments, yet you can always leave a lasting impression that doesn't require you to step into the light.

You are a prominent piece to his riddle, whether he knows it or not. Your purpose is far beyond sexual acts; your level of femininity enhances his masculinity. You are the muse that rejuvenates him when he is drained as you pluck the strings to his guitar, you fulfill roles that others cannot perform; you are the fantasy in his reality and have the power to keep things private and mysterious. You know him in ways that others do not; you keep his secrets, and just being around you gives him an inquiring taste that he just can't put his finger on, yet it's deliciously irresistible.

Side chicks have been around for years. They come in different forms and are often more accessible to gravitate to because she isn't handling the role of his woman. She isn't managing bills, wrangling kids, or dealing with all his different moods, and she doesn't have to. Many have no desire to. Those women know the difference between the side dish and the desert. S/N some people pass on the desert; it's rich and often surpasses their caloric allowance, but some desserts are just too good to pass up.

You can be the coleslaw or the caramel Sunday. The French fries or the apple pie. It's solely up to you, but you are NOT the Steak honey; never forget!

Side chick affirmation of the day!
Say this aloud and repeat it!

"I have the right to remain silent!"
Side chick-alations
5

LAW SIX

Thou Shall Not Seek Vengeance

"For vengeance is an emptiness, and one that seeketh is useless themselves."
Vengeance is not yours 6: 1

Keisha "The Vengeful Side Chick"

Play with fire; you will get burned!

 crolling through my Facebook app, I rolled my eyes at all of the "fakery." In the land of creating your own reality, these creeps act as if we don't know them in real life. Amused, I chuckled and took a bite of my burger.

"Keisha, you have been holding out, I see!"

Catching me off guard, I jolted out of my place of comfort and into attention mode. I hate staying in the break room on lunch. As soon as you get comfortable, you got some rag-a-muffin striking a conversation you aren't interested in having.

"What are you rambling about now, Nicole?" I asked, letting out a long and exasperating breath.

"Oh, you know exactly what I am speaking of, Keisha." Nicole stood 5'1, with her petite little hands on her hip, tapping her size "6" heel against the carpet.

Unmoved and irritated, I glanced at my watch. "Breaks almost over chile, and I am not in the mood to play charades, sis."

Nicole narrowed her eyes and folded her arms across her chest. "Fine! I saw that all-white BMW pull out from the driveway this morning."

I pulled her arm and yanked her closer, tugging her down in the seat across from me. Leaning into her, I looked around the room before speaking in a hushed tone. "You didn't see shit; why in the hell are you so damn nosey all the time, Nickey?"

Nicole and I are first cousins. After a bad breakup with her fiancé and my ex-best friend, Fallyn, and I had a huge falling out, she moved in with me. Letting her crash at my spot was probably the worst mistake I could've made, EVER! But I needed the money to cover Fallyns half.

"Wasn't being nosey. I had to pee."

"The bathroom is nowhere near the window facing the driveway, Nickey.

"I got hungry, damn! Don't try to spin this around on me. I know that car, seen it plenty times before an…."

"And I don't know what car you are speaking of. End of discussion!" I snapped, pushing myself back from the table.

By the time I got home, I had noticed Nicole had made it there first. I walked in the house, and there she was, sitting on the sofa drinking her bitter-ass cup of tea. I hung up my purse and hurried past her. I placed my head on the steering wheel and said a mini prayer before entering the house.

"She gone whoop yo ass! Again!" Nicole scoffed as I walked away.

I stopped in my tracks and took a deep breath, contemplating how I wanted to tell Nicole's whack ass to go to hell with gasoline drawls on, disrespectfully. I hated that I even got her into my company. She is one of those people that will irritate your soul until you jump off a bridge. Even then, she would walk over to the bridge, peer down in the direction of your twisted body, and say, *"now what you go and do that for? Anyways…."*

Nicole can't hold water, she will try, but it won't last long, a perfect dummy for a puppet. She doesn't stop, and there is no off button. This is the sole reason why I told JD he couldn't come through last night. His thirsty behind just wouldn't listen. To be honest, I knew he wouldn't, and it was part of the plan I placed in motion.

Putting on my façade, I took three steps back, turned to face her, and grabbed her hands. "This is why we both know there was no BMW, right? I nodded with a look of concern in my eyes.

Nicole gave me a side-eye and pursed her lips together. "Keisha, this ain't right, girl. You know how much it hurt me when I found out Jason was stepping out on me. To even think that you would go as low to sleep with someone you consider to be a close…."

"Considered!" I snapped. Leave it to Nicole to make this shit all about her someway somehow.

Nicole threw her hands up in the air, "cut the shit! You and Fallyn have been through worse. You two always bounce back. This, this ain't the way!"

"Listen, Nickey, just calm down. You are right, I gotta find a way to fix this, and I just need some time. I know I messed up big time and…" I shook my head and stood up, placing my hands on my head in defeat. I should have gotten a Grammy for this performance chile. It almost topped the performance I gave JD last night. His dick is whack might I add. I had to fake two orgasms and give him head to get the third. You read right. I got more orgasm off giving him head than actually screwing him. How Fallyn managed to stick with it for so long and remain loyal was beyond me. This fool was wearing Nike from head to toe with a dick that just couldn't do it. I even got on top and started fucking him so hard I put *his* legs up.

He was so pissed, *"Now Keisha, you know damn well you don't do no shit like that!"*

Just thinking about it almost ruined my award-winning performance with Nicole.

Scanning my face, Nicole raised a brow, "when did this happen?" she asked.

Her nosey ass couldn't care less about Fallyn; she needed some tea to keep her hydrated and rejuvenated, especially after drinking that bitter shit she was sipping. Some people get off on others' drama, and she was one of those people. I thought back to how it all began, and to be honest, I would do it all again with my eyes closed wide.

It was the day of Fallyn and I's falling out.

"Why would you even think that was ok, Keisha?"

"I was going to give it back, Fallyn. It's not like you don't have it."

"It's the principle. If I have it or not, you don't take anything of mine without asking."

It was a measly ass fifty dollars I borrowed from her wallet. I was going to give it right back as soon as I went to the ATM. Fallyn is loaded with cash, and for some reason, she acts as if me borrowing the money would have put a dent in her pockets. She has this aura about her that wreaks, "I'm better than you." The shit stinks if you ask me. Since the fifth grade, we have been friends, and I have always felt as if we were more competitors than sisters/friends. Anywho, Fallyn had decided she should move out, talking about "this isn't working" like we were breaking up or something.

Long story short, breaking upturned to breaking valuable items as she and I were rolling around like we were wild ass animals.

Who hit first? Me! JD walked in just before Fallyn's fist would connect with my jaw one final time and dragged her off of me. She was leaving me high and dry with no roommate, and she knew damn well, I could barely foot my half.

Two hours had gone by, I was icing my face and deleting her from all of my social media platforms. Looking through her pictures, I immediately felt that maybe she was better than me. I mean, look at her.

"You fat miserable bitch! You gone die with a brownie in your hand; broke and lonely! No man would ever, could ever take your sloppy ass seriously!"

Whenever I complained about my weight, Fallyn would interject. She would say things like, "You are thick, sis," or "You are not even close to fat!" The words cut deep, especially since it was the first time I had heard how she really felt about me.

Now, she tells the truth. She worked out every day and would never eat my food. Who knew that her living with me and looking at my "fat, sloppy ass" would be her motivation to keep in shape?

Tears rolled down my face as I took a large bite of my rice cake. Just as the tears had hit the screen of my phone, I received a notification from JD.

JD: *Hey beautiful, you good?*

I smiled as I wiped the lone tear from my face.

Me: *I am. Thanks for asking.*

JD: *You already know gorgeous…let me ask you something…*

From there, we talked, and I became more prone to showing Fallyn how lonely I would be with her man laying next to my 'fat ass' warm and cozy!

JD set a date in this low-key spot downtown. I got dressed in my see-through leggings, smelling like a million bucks: no panties! I beat my face and laid my hair. A slay like no other.

"So, wait! You did all this for another woman's man? A woman that has been your best friend from childhood and…."

"And yes! Don't judge me, Nicky; I'm tired of Fallyn with her nose in the air like her shit don't stink. And you know what? I like JD. Fallyn doesn't appreciate him one bit. She is a nag, and she complains about everything…."

"Says JD?" Nicole scoffed.

I slammed the fridge and twisted the cap of my soda before taking a long gulp. "Says, facts Nicky! JD is good people; he is just a man being a man, and Fallyn is always setting expectations beyond measures." I contested, rolling my eyes in agitation.

"So *you* decided not to set any, is what you're saying?"

"Here you go, you sound like…."

"A woman with some standards is what I sound like."

"Figures! Leave it to you to think you can look down on me, and you ain't got a pot to piss in either. At the end of the day, I'm enjoying myself, and I'm gone ride this horse till he can't giddy up, you feel me?"

"You bitches disgust me! You are so quick to let a dude slide in you all willy nilly, knowing good and well he ain't gone elevate you to no level beyond bed level. You get off on another woman's man wanting you because you have no morals and self-respect for your damn self. If I were Fallyn, I would leave you leaking wide open, and I ain't talking bout in between yo legs. That thang is dry and smells like someone crawled in it and died. I have been smelling you for two days now, and you need to fix it; instead, you over there trying to break up some shit cause you bitter!"

"Bitter?" I laughed, with my hand over my chest. "Says the same chick that waits until I fall asleep every night to go do a drive-by on a man that left her for the *'cole-slaw'* you call a *'side chick.'* See, all of this misdirected anger stems from you knowing damn well, 'us bitches' have the power to elevate far beyond bed level. Bitch bumped you down to a level that ain't even on the radar if you ask me.."

SLAP

Nicole had slapped me so hard my face burned almost as bad as I felt when I last took a piss.

"Pack yo shit! Get the hell out!" I screamed, holding the side of my face.

"Nah, I'm not going nowhere. Not until my month is up. You gone have to deal with me until then. But you need to go to the clinic with yo funky pussy ass." Nicole scoffed, turning her nose up.

I reached into my crotch, played with my juices, and brought my hand up to my nose. "Smells like roses." I lied. Something was undeniably off, and my pH was definitely off balance. I made a mental note to make an appointment. But tonight, I have a date.

"I can't believe you brought me here." I leaned into JD and spoke in a hushed tone. I looked around the restaurant in awe. No one had ever done something so thoughtful for me. I smoothed out my hair and thought to myself all the ways I would make JD cum tonight.

"Anything for you, princess." He smiled as he rubbed my hand.

We laughed as he gave me all of these smiles and looks that made me feel all warm and fuzzy inside. This wasn't supposed to be happening this way. I wasn't supposed to fall this hard or even at all, for that matter.

We take the long way to his place. He had another spot across town, and he had been dying for me to see it. I let the window down as the breeze blew in my hair as *Trey Songz* song "Disrespectful" serenaded my ears

Girl, you so special, I don't mind bein' disrespectful

Girl, you so special, we're so disrespectful

Girl, you can call my phone at four in the morning

Girl, you can ride shotgun every time I'm rolling

Girl, you can come with me to her favorite diner

She even took me home so I could meet her mama

(disrespectful)

By the time we made it to his spot, his hands were cupping the back of my neck as I took his penis and began to fuck him with my mouth. Leaving no room for air, I kissed it slowly and sensually; he twitched in anticipation. I deep throat him as my salvia soaks him, gripping his balls in one hand and his dick in the other. I twisted and turned, slurped, and moaned. I could feel him throbbing as my vagina moistened.

I couldn't wait any longer as I picked up the pace. JD gripped my hair tightly, trying to slow me down, but it was too late. I went to work on him, and my mouth was a disrespectful savage. It took me less than five minutes to get him to cum, and I refused to let up until I swallowed every baby that swam to shore.

Entering his bedroom, he makes me feel relaxed. He pushes me against the wall and kisses me aggressively.

"Wait, let me go to the bathroom first." I needed to do a smell check before going any further. My pH balance had been completely off, and I have yet to hear back from the clinic.

The bathroom was adjacent to his bedroom; I strolled my way in there before turning to give him a seductive grin. His bathroom was so put together and dainty I second-guessed this being his hideaway spot. The color scheme was so warm and cozy. Not like a bachelor pad at all.

I placed my hand inside my leggings, and before I could bring them back to my nose, I damn near passed out.

"Fuck it!" I hissed. I took a five-minute hoe bath and proceeded with my evening.

JD laid me on his bed and began to kiss me passionately. He kept kissing me down to my lower belly, letting his cheek rest against my thigh. "What do you want?" He whispered, looking me deep into my eyes.

"You," I replied. "Inside of me." I continued in between breaths.

Crawling back up to me, he lifted my lower region into him, kissing me passionately. He flipped me over and entered my cubby hole with force. This time was much different than the last. I loved the way he handled me with aggression, intensity, power. He felt so good inside of me, and even though I knew it wasn't right, I couldn't stop him.

"JD put on a rubber baby!" I moaned.

"Come on, girl, it feels so good; besides, it's too late. He groaned, pounding my insides so good I obeyed him; I couldn't disturb him now; his momentum was just right.

He grips my breast from behind and takes his time; I could feel every inch of him as he throbbed inside of me. I threw it back as he whispered all sorts of obscenities into my ear.

We went on like this for a good 45 mins before we climaxed all over his silk sheets.

After, he exits the room for a bit. I could hear him whispering what seemed to be a disagreement.

I bet that's Fallyn's ass! I thought to myself, smiling connivingly and with satisfaction.

JD brings me a glass of water and tosses my clothes on the bed. The sudden change in energy caught me off guard.

"I thought we were spending the night together?"

"Yeah, I got something I gotta take care of. You need to get dressed like now. Your Uber is on the way."

"Uber? "I snapped.

"Did I stutter?" He retorted before leaving the room hurriedly. "Let's go!" He called over his shoulder.

I got dressed and walked toward the door. JD sat on the sofa drinking a glass of something dark, not even bothering to look at me.

"See you, tomorrow babe." He didn't reply.

———————— ❧ ————————

The next day, I walked through the mall looking for something to wear to this Halloween party. JD's dubious behavior bothered me, and he didn't even bother to call and make sure I had made it home safely. My mind raced as I tried to piece together what happened last night.

"Keisha?" a familiar voice chirped from behind.

I turned to see Fallyn looking as stunning as ever, skin glowing and all. My childhood friend greeted me with a warm and long hug.

"How have you been?" She smiled. "I miss you, friend."

Instantly, I was overcome by guilt, and I could barely even put together a sentence without stuttering. "I... I have been great, Fallyn." I lied. I was miserable.

"Keesh, I just want to apologize to you for everything. See, JD had been stealing from me, and everything about that situation had drained my very being. To the point where it filtered into my other relationships, including ours. I should have never allowed that to happen."

With every word she spoke, there was a pain in the pit of my stomach. *Stealing? Why on earth did he need to steal from.*

"I also want you to know that I forgive you." She spoke, catching me off guard. Nicole told me everything, and even though I should be mad at you; Or even wanna whoop yo ass, I can't. Because I know what comes with him is far worse than any ass-whooping anyone can give. He comes with an ass whooping that will burn and suck you dry." She spoke so calmly as my heart raced.

"You thought you were getting back at me?" She chuckled.

Before I could reply, a guy appeared and grabbed her by the hand.

"Good babe?" He asked, his baritone voice demanding notice.

"I am." She smiled, her eyes still fixed on me. "More than I have ever been." She continued. He kissed her on the cheek and walked off, not too far but far enough that he couldn't hear our conversation.

Fallyn tilted her head to the side. "Understand this, Keisha, if he is fucking with you today, or any day for that matter, it's because I'm *not* fucking with him. I control your turn bitch. Tag your it!" She sneered before brushing past me, leaving me to stand in my shit.

The ringing of my phone startled me.

"Hello?"

"Hello Ms. Mitchell, this is the nurse from the Health Department. You must come into our office right away.

\#\#\#

The nerve of this clown to be ignoring me. He is active on his Facebook account, and he has left me on "read" for the past week. Going to message him again, I notice...

"That's weird. I just saw JD's page; where did it go?" that's when it hit me; he blocked me. I become enraged and sick to my stomach as I think back to what I had just heard.

"I'm sorry, you have Chlamydia and Syphilis!" I buried my face in my hands and cried hysterically.

On my drive home, I was flooded with a slew of emotions, fear, confusion, hopelessness. I pull into my driveway and bang my head against the steering wheel as I mumble a prayer. I look up as the Goddess awaits!

Goddess

"If I had a friend like you, I would hate to be your enemy. Since the fifth grade, you hated Fallyn when Brandon Jones picked her over you to take to the school dance. Instead of talking to her, you envied her, allowing envy to fester inside you like the diseases you now carry.

Fallyn has always been loyal to you; in fact, she actually looked up to you more than you know. You allowed your insecurities and malicious

When you dare to screw another woman's man, the least you can do is know how to fight, consult Mr. Miyagi, take some kickboxing classes, something! Not only are you ill-equipped to fight, but you have lost the battle in the vicious cycle of self-love and respect.

However, somewhere along the line, you lost your marbles, made a sound choice to seek vengeance, and create the idiotic narrative that you're justified to sleep with this thieving burning ass negro. JD ain't shit, on any level beyond broke and irresponsible!

Vengeance has clouded your mind as usual, and you have found yourself in a jam, which you always do. All because you were so focused on hurting Fallyn that you ignored all the red flags and failed to do a fact check and run a credit report on his penis, now you are over there leaking and stinking like a damn dead fish in a pond.

Vengeance is not yours 6: 1 *'For vengeance is an emptiness, and one that seeketh is useless themselves.'*

Mustn't you agree there is no room for vengeance in this game? Furthermore, revenge is not nor has it ever been yours to inflict on anyone, which is why you are covered with skin rashes, swollen lymph nodes, and a mound of lesions. Don't whine! Do better! You have played with fire and will now burn in the pits of hell!

Burn Baby Burn!"

DAILY READ!

hough one can certainly understand the anger and disappointment that would motivate someone to get back at someone, vengeance has no place in *Side Chick Paradise*. Vengeance is a sure way into a pissing contest to see who can urinate the highest, the farthest, for the longest. It is a waste of time and energy that serves no purpose. In fact, it takes a psychological and physical toll on you, and though It may give you an invigorating feeling, it doesn't last!

Side chick-ism is not to intentionally hurt someone you are angry with, jealous of or whatever else. If you have an issue with another individual, it's best to communicate that to the individual instead of waiting until the boiling point. Even if you don't know what you're mad about yet, you can have that conversation.

One of the advantages of being a side chick is that you get all the benefits with little drama. A side chick doesn't nag, doesn't ask questions, and most definitely doesn't seek vengeance.

Once you come to grips with not being the main in his life without feeling used, you will see how you get all of the great perks from a "relationship" with none of the headache. But if you are here for vengeance, you will be sucked in the past, dwelling on your own sorrows, defusing misery as you move.

Being hurt by others is very painful, and it leaves a stain, but these stains speak of your trials and triumphs against the grinding of life. Whatever happened, happened in the past. Let bygones be bygones and move on, chin up, head high because you might have tripped, you might have fallen, but you got up and marched forward.

**Side chick affirmation of the day!
Say this aloud and repeat it!**

"There is no room for vengeance in this game."
Side chick-alations
6

LAW SEVEN
Thou Shall Not Think They Are Exempt
"Thy humility is the greatest quality that man shalt have, and arrogance is unquestionably the most repulsive."

Thy tables will turn7:1

Emerald "The Overly Confident Side Chick"
Cocktails and Concoctions

"I don't understand Emmy like I do everything! I cook, I clean I.."

"Talk too damn much, Sierra! What man do you think wants to hear nagging and whining all the time about what you do for them?"

"It's not that, I just feel like he doesn't see my efforts, and I know he's messing around."

"What? How do you know that?"

She took a deep breath and exhaled. "I saw the messages in his phone."

"Since when are we going through phones, CiCi? I told you, leave the investigation to me. Why are you so damn hard-head? Have you been taking your…"?

"Don't Emmy! I am not crazy, and you are not the only one that knows how to investigate some shit." She hiccuped after taking a drink.

"Put the damn cup down and go take a long shower! Get yourself together. Go and pull out the sexiest lingerie you have, hell wait….."

I texted my assistant for a quick emergency rescue before returning to the call. I looked around before speaking firm and getting straight to the point. "Listen, you are not even thirty days into the marriage yet, and I don't know how much you would even get from him in such a short time. You got yourself into this shit; now you are going to stick it out until you have invested enough time for us to clean his ass out."

"Who said anything about leaving?"

"Well, what the hell are you snooping for Sierra? Damn!"

I rubbed my temples and allowed the thoughts in my head to drown out the sound of my sister's voice. I don't understand women like her. I love her, but I don't get it. Women will be a man's girlfriend for a decade and overlook all of the bull he puts her through, and as soon as they get married, they start seeing "oh so clearly" now. I don't want any parts in her newfound vision.

Women are so basic and act as if keeping a man is complicated, which is why some of these women aren't worthy of a man. Furthermore, they don't know how to treat him.

But me? I do! Which is something I know all too well. Trust and believe, a wise man isn't going to leave behind what he knows he won't find again, which is why I designed an agency that educates women on how to obtain and keep their man.

Yes! I've been married for 18 years. My high school sweetheart, Roderick, made me his wife, his one and only. He won't even look in another woman's direction, let alone cheat.

"Mrs. Craig, he's ready for you." The receptionist's voice rang in, kicking my sister's whining back in as well.

"Sierra, I have to go. I have a meeting. Love you, bye."

My heels clicked against the marble floors. I followed behind the receptionist, eying her from head to toe. She modestly sashays her way to the office. Her jet-black hair was held up with a checkered headband that matched her long sleeve bodycon dress that stopped right before hitting her well-toned calves, which were accentuated by her sheer tights adorned with a large black stripe up the middle of her shins.

Stopping at the office door, I watch as she gives herself a self-check before knocking, smoothing out her hair, exposing a bit more cleavage, and…

"Ahem!" I interrupt, reminding her why she was at the door in the first place.

She froze in place as a mild flush crept across her already rosy cheeks. I gave her a friendly smile and a head nod assuring her that I understood all too well. She let out a breath of relief and excused herself abruptly. Mr. Chambers was very easy on the eye, and men like him were hard to come by and even harder to keep on a leash.

I strode into the office and stood as I watched briefly. He faced the large window peering at the beautiful view. Closing the door behind me, I cleared my throat.

"Mrs. Emerald Craig!" He spoke over his shoulder. His voice was soothing yet, authoritative.

"Thanks for coming by." He stated, now turning to face me,

I could only see his mouth moving as my focus had been seized by the man walking towards me. Purpose blazing from his light green eyes, he took every breath I had to give, and it took me 1.2 seconds to breathe again.

"Thanks for seeing me." I graced him with a smile.

"My Pleasure, and please call me David."

Again, I heard nothing, but extremely grateful I could read lips. I told myself to look away, but David was oh so mesmerizing. Charming eyes and a sexy five O'clock shadow perfectly framed his squared-off jawline and prominent chin; medium height and excellent build and the most distinguished vanilla man I had ever laid eyes on.

Let's not forget, a very successful partner in an accounting firm and one of the most prominent men in the firm that had just written one of the largest checks to hit my bank account to date. Mind your business, don't count my pockets, and let's stick to the subject at hand.

Why was I here?

I took the check out of my purse and set it on his desk. "I can't take this, Mr..... I mean David. Conflict of interest."

The fact of the matter is, David also happens to be the CEO of the largest PI firm in Ohio. He was looking for me to be an addition to his team. I ran my own private firm that aims to help women catch their man doing dirt and take him to the cleaners after. I was compelled to add a bonus to teach them what they are doing wrong to make their men roam.

"Would you like a drink?"

I raised an eyebrow, "I don't know if I should under these conditions."

"Under these conditions, you should." He insisted while pouring me a drink.

"It's the good stuff, I can assure you." He said, handing me the glass.

I brought it up to my lips as he watched, seeming to enjoy the scene while resting his body against his desk. Not to mention he was....

"Does she know?"

"She knows something, but what? That remains a mystery."

"A mystery, I trust you will.."

"David cut the shit and fuck me before I fuck you first." sinfully sexy.

I love my husband. I really do. But Roderick is nowhere near in the same league as this man who has my legs wrapped around his waist while mounted on top of his desk. There is something quite unusual about him and though I knew what I was doing was far below my moral compass, but...

"Sssss..." He exhaled as I guided him inside me. Once deep inside, I began a slow rotation of my hips. He grew larger inside me, harder emboldened by the warmth of my vagina. I wrapped my legs tighter as he gripped my throat, gauging his masterstrokes to the shaking of my knees as I began to cum for the third time.

He stopped in time, lifting me off the desk and bringing me to my knees. He gripped the back of my neck and laid his penis in my palm. I wrapped my lips around his peach-colored manhood and closed my lips around it as I squeezed on it tightly, sliding it in and out of my mouth relentlessly until he released his last droplets of orgasm into my mouth. After he finished, I stopped time, cleanse him off with my travel towelettes, and exited gracefully.

I hadn't put my key into the ignition well before my phone rang, displaying the name; I was beginning to resent more now than ever.

"Cindy…" I sang, rolling my eyes.

"I need to see you. Meet me in the morning; I will send the address later this evening."

"Cindy, I already told you…."

"It's urgent; I won't ask again!" The phone clicked, enraging me.

The nerve of this prissy bitch to…Oops, where are my manners? I forgot to add, David's third finance in the past two years, Cindy had hired me to investigate her future husband and his endeavors, she had a hunch. I investigated alright and fell dead smack onto his peach dick as he rocked my fucking world.

I can't tell you how I managed to be the side chick to a man all while married, but I can tell you that this shit has been going on for a whole three months, and I was risking it all! This was nothing new to David; a woman couldn't keep this man to save her life.

However, the connection between David and I was beyond simple sexual pleasure. It was something special, and we both knew it

Before I could catch my breath, my phone rang again. Yet this time, I was hit with a sense of adoration and guilt at the same damn time.

"Hey Emmy, my flight was delayed and..."

"Delayed? Til when Rod? I have an important meeting in the morning. I can't be out too late."

"I know, and I wouldn't dare ask you too. I already called David, he is going to pick me up from the airport, and we are going to have drinks and watch the game at the sports bar later…I'll sleep in the guest room tonight so that I won't wake you."

The sound of that name did something to me. Oh yea, I guess you can say the plot thickens. David is also my husband's best friend. Yea, I know. Roderick is the best man any woman could ever ask for. He is loyal, caring, and a damn good and faithful husband. Dave is not, however, in the same league as my husband, maybe not in the same species. He is…. David and David are naughty, and there ain't nothing nice about him.

he following morning, I sat at the table in the far back of the restaurant downstairs from this beautiful hotel across town. I sipped my coffee as Cindy stormed in five minutes after I arrived, disheveled and inconspicuous.

"You lied to me!" She snapped, slamming a manilla envelope on the table. Looking over her shoulders, she pulled out her chair and plopped down instinctively.

"What the hell are you talking about, Cindy? And why in the hell are you are acting paranoid?"

"He's going to leave me; I know it!" She cried, burying her face into her hands.

See, this is what I'm talking about. Women have no clue how to keep their men happy or satisfied. They do the bare minimum and wonder why they end up in a state where they keep their head on a swivel and remain distrustful; who wants to live like that, huh?

She stopped the crying fest and gave me a scowl that could have annihilated Lucifer. "Paranoid? Emmy, I saw it with my own damn eyes."

I swallowed hard. I swear I had been discreet; *I knew I shouldn't have fucked that man in that office. Dammit!* I cursed myself.

"Emerald! Are you listening? I did my own investigating and…"

"I can explain…I.."

"It's not your fault. I wouldn't have found it had it not been for me finding David's backup phone."

Backup phone? I don't…. I never knew of a backup phone.

"I went through it, and the messages read, *"we are on for tonight; meet me at our spot."* So, I tracked the phone, leading me here; I saw him pull up. I watched as he walked around the car and opened the door for her. I couldn't see her face, but I took pictures. I went across the street and printed them out…."

My heart was racing. I, too, had felt betrayed at this moment. Even though David is not my problem, part of me feels like he is.

"I have the key." She whispered.

"How the…"

"Now is not the time Emmy." She snapped before getting up from the table and walking towards the elevator.

I followed behind, just as curious as she was. After getting on the elevator, I slowly opened the manilla folder and braced myself.

My mind began to race as I suddenly remembered. "Why would Rod cover for him?"

"What?"

"Rod. He said he and David were going out for drinks and."

"That's what friends do, Emerald. They cover for one another and lie about it."

"No, not my man. There must be more to it. Are you sure it was…"?

"Look at the pictures, Emmy!" She jeered.

The elevator opened before pulling out the pictures, and Cindy stormed off. I stormed behind her, now even more infuriated. As Whitney Houston's "Saving all my Love" resounded through the doors, we both stood still.

A few stolen moments is all that we shared
You've got your family, and they need you there
Though I try to resist, being last on your list
But no other man's gonna do

So I'm saving all my love for you...

My heart sank as I pulled the pictures out from the envelope. I looked at the pictures long and hard but, something wasn't right about this.

That dress, that dress, and those shoes. I thought.

Cindy put the key card in and pushed the door open. My heart sank as they both lay there naked with sly smirks spread across their face.

"Rod! What the hell?"

Goddess

This was one of those times where I was speechless, my damn self. I stood in disbelief briefly as the heat in the kitchen had been turned all the way up!

"Alexa, call out everyone in the closet! And play *R Kelly's,* 'Trapped in the Closet' while you're at it." I shouted. "This shit show is more than, even I, can bear to watch." I laughed as I stood next to Mrs. High Horse ass Emerald.

"Isn't that the dress and heels you've been looking for the past few days? "The look on her face was priceless, "How did one not suspect this one, my dear? Aren't you the one that said women need to do their part! And I quote, 'fuck him till his soul leaves his body, nourish him, fuck him again till he has nothing left to give.' Your motto was quite simple, right?

You sat on your high horse and chastised other women as you gloated about how it is not as complicated as society makes it appear to make your man 'not cheat' with another woman, that is. No pun intended.

The thing is, some people believe they are champagne in a tall glass. When in all actuality, they're lukewarm piss in a plastic cup.

The arrogant, judgmental, and egotistical appear to think they are better than you. The truth is they are attempting to convince themselves that they are. Need I remind you, "humility" is the greatest quality that man shalt have, and arrogance is unquestionably the most repulsive."

Which is why you failed to see what was right in front of your face. That your dear and faithful husband had no interest in any other woman because, well, even the blind can see; this was no one time spur of the moment thing, nor was it fulfilling a fantasy. It looks like you were fucking not one, but two, *Rectum Rangers*.

This, my dear, was an ongoing relationship. Being that David and Cindy are not married and you broke your own marital agreement with *your* husband by sleeping with another man, which, might I add, was all a part of their strategic plan, you will not reap the benefits of the divorce. Needless to say, he wins either way. I guess you have to develop a new motto, but mines remain.

Burn in hell!"

DAILY READ!

here is no exact art behind keeping a man from cheating or any individual for that matter. Because affairs are so easy to cover up, how can one know that they are exempt from their partner adding someone else into the equation? Nothing could be done about the three individuals' suppressed feelings in the story above. Everyone had their own logic behind their illogical (from the perception of others) actions.

Dealing with infidelity is more common than one would like to admit and face it; there isn't any specific sexually-that you indicate with a checkmark here. There isn't a "straight" way to do it, nor is there a "gay" way. Like it or not, a cocktail of the two has the same unpleasant flavor.

Many couples are impacted by unfaithfulness; countless pressures include sex addictions, childhood issues, and personality disorders. Not to mention, the influence of social media and inadequate boundaries can boost the likelihood that one of these reasons will lead to some type of affair.

In a perfect world, where there is no such thing, two people will continuously grow at the same pace. The matter is that people constantly change and evolve into something different each day in this life. It's not to say the person cheating doesn't respect the commitment, lacks compassion, or simply doesn't care about the consequences. Perhaps the straying partner had outgrown the relationship or had second thoughts about taking things to the next level, yet they could not convey these sentiments.

TY NESHA

As a side chick, please don't get the game twisted; it is not your job to change him, nor are you exempt from *his* acts against *her*. Don't flatter yourself with fallacies that you hold the potion that will whip this man into the shape, and he would forever be loyal to you. Don't you ever for a second underestimate the role of a woman; his woman.

The side chick life is the rhythm without the blues. You are the 20, and she is the 80. The 20 doesn't require much effort; it's all fun, games, and no pressure. This is not a competition or an audition, nor is it an opportunity to toot your own horn and tear her down. Don't get ahead of yourself and sign up to fill the shoes that don't fit your unswollen feet.

You also must know who you are dealing with. The truth is, a good woman, a good side chick, a good person overall, can't keep a man. The only thing that will make a man faithful is a man that chooses to do so by putting down his player's card.

To some men, cheating is a sport, and in that case, you can be a five-star woman and still crave a happy meal. They're deep in their bad habits and will not change them. At least not anytime soon; a tiger doesn't change its stripes no matter how good you are to him. After all, if you fill her position, yours is now open.

Side chick affirmation of the day!
Say this aloud and repeat it!

"Be humble, or I will be humbled."
Side chick-alations
8

Thou Shall Always Stay Aware

"Thy mustn't expect to drift naively through life without grief, opposition, or betrayal, and surely not to be forsaken.

Be nobody's fool 1:8

Jennifer "The Clueless Side Chick"

Never creep, where you sleep

I was finally settled in at my new place. I could finally pour myself a drink, put my feet up, and...

Ding Dong

Now I just moved in, so I don't know who will be ringing my doorbell. On top of that, it is way past my bedtime. I took a peep out to peephole, and lo and behold...

"Eric? What are you doing here?" I asked, opening the door.

He stumbled in and pushed past me.

"Ewe, you smell like dead fish in a barrel on a hot day!" I scoffed, Eric reeked of alcohol, and I hated when he got this way.

"She broke up with me." He whined, his words slurring.

Rolling my eyes, I let out a breath of frustration mixed with relief. "What's new? You guys break up like every week." I murmured, closing the door behind him.

"Well, this time, it is for good," he insisted, plopping down on my sofa.

"Thank God!" I thought to myself. This was his fifth breakup with Michelle, and he insisted that this time was the last, but he swore that the last time and even then, he walked around in a lugubrious condition for months.

I watched him slump down like a bum in the streets. I wanted so bad to rinse him off with a water hose, but instead, I squeezed my nose and pulled him up with my free hand.

"Oh no, you don't! Shower! Now!" I ordered, pushing him towards the bathroom.

As soon as he entered the bathroom, I collapsed over the arm of the couch and rolled my eyes. I took a deep breath and tried to push down the all too familiar feeling I got every time Eric came around. My love for him was unmatched, and he refused to see me. Instead, he did things you would do to a baby sister, like pat the top of my head or lick the tip of his thumb and wipe the corner of my mouth. He never looked at me the way I looked at him, and he never will.

"It's just for one night, Jennifer," I said to myself.

No sooner than the words escaped my mouth, Eric exited the bathroom with a towel wrapped around his lower region. His chiseled abs glistened. Eric was a sight to behold, a work of art, especially when his lean 6'1 frame stood in front of me partially naked. I counted backward as I took it all in *"10, 9, 8..."*

"Jenny! Are you listening?"

"Huh? Wha?"

"I may need to crash here for a few weeks, just until I...."

"Did he just say, a few weeks? How am I supposed to do that? I can't live with this man for..."

"It's okay if you can't. I can stay with my parents, but...."

"No, it's cool, Eric. Of course, you can stay." If I could go back

81

and do it again, I probably would have done it the same way. Even though I was heading down a tunnel of darkness with my eyes opened wide.

The Morning After

I opened my eyes, and with a slight turn of my head, I winced when I noticed him lying there.

"Fuck," I whispered as I bought my hand up to my mouth.

I climbed out of bed, trying not to wake him; I tipped toed my way into the bathroom and looked at myself in the mirror. My light blue eyes had a sparkle that I'd never seen before. Smoothing out my curls, I pushed my hair up into a messy bun. I gripped the sink and lowered my head in infamy. *What had I just done? Had I really slept with my best friend?* I thought to myself.

I could hear Eric awaking; I took a deep breath. "Eric, we need to…."

Before finishing my statement, I felt a firm grip around my waist. "Eric, last night…."

"Was amazing." He whispered before kissing my neck gently. His lips were so soft. I could still smell the alcohol seeping out his pores. He reached into the shower and turned on the water. I stood there frozen in thought.

I didn't know how to say this, but it needed to be said. "Last night shouldn't have happened; we were really drunk and…."

Before I could finish, Eric gripped the nape of my neck with one hand and inserted himself inside of me with the other. My back arched as he stroked me passionately. Stopping in time, he walked me to the shower; I stepped in and stepped back to allow the showerhead to spray him with beads that draw attention to his strong shoulders, gleam off his arms and trickle down his rib cage.

A splash of water strikes my face as I am dazed out of my musing. My eyes then travel down to his oh so beautiful penis. It is the same tropical almond color as the rest of his body. His dick was super thick and made my mouth water. The type of thick I wanted to dominate with my mouth and pussy.

His arms gripped around me as he spun me around and pressed himself against me. My head lowers as my hands push against the tile. He parts my legs and enters me. I bite my bottom lip as a moan escapes my mouth while he grips my well-rounded 36C- cup breasts and twists my nipples, driving me crazy.

I could feel his dick growing so big inside me. Launching into my cries of ecstasy, he drove himself harder into me as I whined with pleasure, climaxing again instantly.

He continued, slowing himself; I could feel him throbbing inside me as I pulsated against him. He grunted as he came, I tried to stop him, but it was too late. He gripped my waist and pulled me back in, and I had cum again; he rested his head against my back as we separated shakily.

"Jenny, you didn't!"

I frowned, "and that's a bad thing?"

"Uh, yeah," She blurted out. "Or no. Hell, I don't know Jenny! He was vulnerable and…."

"And what? You don't think I'm good enough?"

"What? No. I mean, that's not what I'm saying."

In fact, that's exactly what she was saying. Eric had never looked at me in that way. He always liked girls like Michelle. The type of girls that were supper prissy and uppity; wore skimpy clothes and were simply irresistible. Not girls like myself, girls that wore oversized flannels and sweats; girls that wore messy buns and never went to the salon.

It had been three months already, and not only was Eric still living in my house, but he had also become very withdrawn. Anytime I would call, his phone would ring once and go straight to voicemail. He never wanted to hang out outside of these four walls and the sex; well, the sex had become rather dull.

Who knew that dating the man I have loved most of my life would be this boring?

I walked out of the dressing room, and Samantha's eyes widened.

"OMG! Jennifer. You…you look…."

"Is it that bad? I knew this was a bad idea!"

Samantha spun me around, and I didn't even notice the girl, no, the woman staring back at me. This was the first time; I saw myself since we started. It was my golden 25th birthday, and my girl bestie insisted on getting me a makeover from head to toe.

The short lace dress with a revealing neckline hugged my body, highlighting curves I didn't even know existed. It was everything for me, my hair, my makeup. Everything!

"Ooh, ooh, ooh, ooh."

Samantha stopped in her tracks, waved her hands in the air, and pulled me into her, singing *Adele's* "Rumor" as it blared over the speakers in the clothing store.

> *She, she ain't real*
> *She ain't gon' be able to love you like I will*
> *She is a stranger*
> *You and I have history, or don't you remember?*
> *Sure, she's got it all*
> *But baby, is that really what you want?*

This was our favorite song, and to me, it related more now than ever. She passed me the invisible mic as I took it home,

> *Bless your soul, you've got your head in the clouds*
> *She made a fool out of you and, boy, she's bringin' you down*
> *She made your heart melt, but you're cold to the core*
> *Now rumor has it, she ain't got your love anymore*

We sang in unisons as we danced and spun in circles,

> *Rumour has it (Rumour)*
> *Rumour has it (Rumour)*

Rumour has it (Rumour)

Rumour has it (Rumour)

Rumour has it (Rumour)

Rumour has it (Rumour)

Rumour has it (Rumour)

"Rumour has it!" We laughed and fell into one another but were interrupted by applause given by the small crowd that had accumulated around us. I hadn't smiled this hard in the past few weeks, and it was long overdue.

"Well, all I have to say is, Eric, is going to fall at your feet, darling," Samantha said, with her hand on my shoulder.

"Maybe." My eyes lowered, "he... he...he didn't come home last night. Or the night before."

"What? Where the hell was he?" Sam asked, crossing her arms.

"I asked him that this morning when he finally decided to make his way through the door. He said he stayed out late with the guys and crashed at Brandon's place. Then, he kissed me on my forehead, ran up the stairs, and hopped in the shower."

"And? Do you believe him?"

"I don't know what to believe, Samantha. He didn't even say happy birthday!"

She waved her hand dismissively, "worry about that another time, today is your day, and we are going to make the best of it." She smiled, pulling me in for a hug.

The day passed without incident, and at sunset, I would finish off my day with the man I loved oh so dearly.

I had just walked through the door of my apartment when my phone rang

"Hey there, Sunshine." Eric's voice rang out, sending shudders through my body.

A smile overtook my face. I loved it when Eric called me that. Suddenly, a sick feeling rose inside of me. I went up to the bedroom, and the moment I stepped through the door, my stomach spun.

"Uh, hey Jenny, happy birthday, you remember Michelle, my…."

"Fiancé." She intervened, showing the large diamond in her hand.

At that moment, Olivia Rodrigo's words to the song "Traitor" played in the back of my head

Brown guilty eyes and little white lies
Yeah, I played dumb, but I always knew
That you talked to her, maybe did even worse
I kept quiet, so I could keep you

And ain't it funny
How you ran to her
The second that we called it quits?

And ain't it funny
How you said you were friends?
Now it sure as hell don't look like it
You betrayed me
And I know that you'll never feel sorry
For the way I hurt, yeah

My chest tightened, and the entire floor disintegrated, taking me down with it

The Goddess

She let out a large gasp as her eyes flew open. She quickly sat up.

"Chile, are you okay?" I placed my hand on her arm.

"Where am I?"

"In the ER," I confirmed, sitting at the edge of the bed.

"Who are you?" She asked, quite disheveled.

"I guess I can't expect you to know where you were when the only contract you signed was one of pure bliss and naivety. Eric was none other than a temporary roommate, and he used his dick for monthly compensation. Have you not ever heard of the saying, never creep, where you sleep?

I threw my hands up. The truth is, I feel sorry for you. You saw all the red flags, yet you still assumed. Assumed, this emotionally stunted, man-child would go off into the wind on a shimmering white horse with you. And let's face it!"

"You don't even like him all that much anymore! You got comfortable with being miserable because you felt that he would fill an unyielding void you didn't know you had. An emptiness transferred to desperation.

You jumped at the opportunity that he and his terrible girlfriend had broken up for the umpteenth time and slid in, no questions asked, all while lowering your standard, trying so hard to pull him up to your level; but he didn't want that, he likes the bottom. He's her bitch, trust me. You might not get to keep the friendship, but you will get to keep the gift, the gift of knowing the universe did you a huge favor by not giving you what you thought you wanted.

Be nobody's fool 1:8 *"Thy mustn't expect to drift naively through life without grief, opposition or betrayal, and surely not to be forsaken."* You must always be aware of your choices and pay attention to what is right in front of you, and if a man does not confirm that he is your one and only, never assume he is. I won't send you to hell this time, but please know, if there ever is another time, you will…

Burn in hell!

DAILY READ!

The shock of finding out that you are a side chick and not knowing it is like paying a debt you don't owe for a situation you didn't buy. You start to wonder what vibe you gave off to be the objective in this game. The pretty picture you once painted is now a distorted image and your newfound reality. You feel the wind knocked out of you unpredictably with an unspoken antagonism on your emotions, and you are overtaken by the insecurities and unanswered questions. *Was I just in the wrong place at the wrong time? Am I not worth being his one and only?* Leading you into a game tug of war with your desires and morals.

Let me be the one to say his actions and decisions have absolutely nothing to do with who you are and everything to do with who he is and will continue to be. Many people hate on the side chick or shift the blame. When in all actuality, they're just as clueless as to the partner that got cheated on. In this era, a culture has been created that makes it difficult to tell if you are a side item because men have mastered the art of deception and perfected their ability to alter their traits to fit whoever they want to catch. I call these men "the pretenders."

The signs have been shown to you, and you need to proceed with your intuition. Understand if the situation started with dishonesty, there would be more to follow. Be careful with those who could potentially try to butter you up. There can always be a balance, but don't go off the deep end for someone who has ulterior motives. Remember the story in the Bible about Eve and the serpent, who tempted her to eat the fruit. Whenever you feel like something is off, stop and think and take what they say at face value. "Watch the snakes because they are watching you."

Side chick affirmation of the day!
Say this aloud and repeat it!

"Choose the game; don't let the game choose you."
Side chick-alations
8

LAW NINE
Thou Shall Not Destroy thy Credit

"The desire of gold is not for gold. It is for the means of independence and benefit. Thy shall not allow one's desires and greed to lead them into bankruptcy."
Credit Denied 9:1-2

Danielle "The Over Seasoned Side Chick"
Dipped in Gold

I took a sip from my glass, leaned over the terrace in my black plush robe, peering down at the view from the balcony of my stunning, two-story, five-bedroom, four-bathroom house. I loved my house. Though I hated that it was hidden away off a country road simultaneously, it stood out with a distinctive, large, planted tree in front. I hated that damn tree. It reminded me of my life and the contract I had signed with only one way out.

I looked down at my phone for the tenth time. Still no text back from Sean. I shook my head in annoyance and sucked my teeth. "This fool got me messed up, and he mustn't have a clue who I am. One thing about me, Ima get another nigga. This is the Heartbreak Hotel; as for him, he most definitely gotta pay." I scoffed, thinking back to how I'd got here in the first place.

Two years prior

After breaking up with who I'd thought to be my life partner at 15, I gave up on Kim and Kanye's relationship goals and decided to "fuck-up". What I mean by that is I found my newfound love on the good ole Internet when my girl Karina put me on to the only fans and IG wagon. When I first started, it was like I was attending a huge party I wasn't even invited to, but I still had to show up every day.

After a few months, it became apparent that my followers couldn't get enough of me, and just like that, I took the Internet by storm. By the time I reached 21, I was more prevalent than agency-signed models earned millions of followers, brand deals, and magazine covers for posting flawless selfies.

You wouldn't believe the type of love I was shown from people who could never even have the pleasure of touching me. By the time I reached 25, I had learned how far beauty and wits could take me. I despised love, and it sickened me to see how twisted these mutha-fuckas were. I refused to conform to someone's pathetic ass girlfriend just to spend every waking day miserable with insecurities. I learned the game and became more strategic.

By 27, I upgraded from an industry hoe and unreformed side chick to a woman who got a nut off exposing niggas and getting away with it. For me, it paid off in more ways than one could imagine. I learned that money is a terrible master but an excellent servant. They paid for my education and provided me with the lifestyle I needed to live. A fashionista in her late 20s who had no desire to fill any shoes unless they were nine-inch stilettos and a graduate student striving to have it all.

"I don't understand why anyone would want to be a side chick. Like women don't respect one another if you asked me." One of the girls in the salon scoffed.

"As long as he's not married, he's fair game." Another one spoke.

"Married or not, it's trashy if you ask me." Girl one retorted.

"Well, good thing no one asked you." She snapped, folding her arms across her chest.

"Well, I'll speak anyways! Side chicks are useless; he will never wife her, never

TY NESHA

leave his woman, and not only is she being played but playing herself."

"I'm starting to think humans aren't meant to be monogamous." Girl three chimed in.

"Not that they're not meant to be. Most people are selfish nowadays and too lazy to make sure it works. I can't trust anyone. Technology ruined it." Girl one continued.

"You are naive. That will be some…."

My stylist spun my chair around just in time, exposing my face to the girls. They gasped and put their hands over their mouths as if they had just said a bad word and their mother walked into the room, catching them red-handed.

The small town we lived in, word got around quickly, and these bitches knew precisely who I was and what I did for a living. The "unapologetic homewrecker" is what they called me.

The name had grown on me because I didn't give a flying shit about a relationship, and I could care less about a married man. When I was twelve, the first married man I ever knew stuck his dick in my mouth and paid me to keep quiet. I held his secret and squeezed him dry until he was on his death bed and confessed to his sister. If you ask me, money rules everything, and I have adopted the "fuck you; pay me" motto from that point on.

I raised an eyebrow and scanned the room before schooling these simple-minded imbeciles. "Society has lied to women, so it will be hard to grasp that all 'side chicks' are not being played. Heck, some are high vital players." I chuckled and stood to my feet, handing my stylist a 100-dollar tip.

"Some women do not want nor value titles. They value fulfilling all aspects of their lives in every way. Most women will never grasp that due to socialization, so you have an uphill battle. You ladies clearly have a lot to learn, but that is what life is about. Don't let your ego make you a fool; It is better to keep your mouth closed and let people think you are a fool than to open it and remove all doubt."

I removed a bundle of cash from my handbag, peeled off the rubber band, and placed fifty dollars in "girl number two's" hand. "I learned early on to be valuable, not available; control what you can, ignore the rest." I ended before tossing my hair back a wink before exiting the salon.

Let me start by stating I am not suggesting women date, screw, or even marry merely for money. However, I do not believe in love and commitment as a solid

92

foundation for anything; tell me, when was the last time you paid a bill with love?

I'll wait!

"Fucking-up" for me is like running a corporation. A business venture: you have to go into it knowing that it could fail or succeed beyond your wildest dreams and make you rich. I graduated from rappers and ballplayers to Politicians, CFO's, Mayors, the top dogs that had far more to lose than their "precious women." They had reputations to uphold, and if they didn't share the vision, believe in it, and work together, the endeavor would fail, and I would indeed expose their ass.

My mom's last dying wish was for me to settle down and have kids; by the time I reached my thirties. I was a 30-year-old savage who liked to devour men of stature. I'd charm them, use them, and then discard them when I got bored. I became bored quickly, which was beneficial because they weren't worthy of me to stick around. I had it all figured out and made it extremely far, but it all came sinking when I met Sean Hansen.

"Girl, who in the entire fuck goes out on a Wednesday?" I asked Karina, irritated that she had dragged me out to this low-key penthouse gathering across town.

"Because Wednesday's is the night where it all goes down."

I hated to admit it, but she was right. This spot was flooded with opulence, and my hands started itching the instant I walked through the door, and I was eager to meet some new prospects. I gut felt this would be a memorable and extravagant night for me. I could hardly contain my excitement as I followed the Karina through the labyrinth of silk-adorned tables, each crowned with a single candle and enclosed by, The lifestyle of the rich and famous.

A mob of crystal blue eyes against China's white skin turned curious gazes in my focus, no doubt wondering who the hell I was, being that my melanin skin was one of only a few in the entire penthouse.

Then there he was, leaned back in the cut, looking like a million bucks.

"Who is that?" I asked Karina, not taking my eyes off him.

"Trouble…" Karina spat and stormed off, leaving me in the middle of the room.

The ambiance was absolutely set for amenity, and I blended right in with my royal blue velvet gown paired with silver bedazzled shoulder detailing, which hugged each curve of mine along with sparkly thigh-high boots. A gift from one of my men, of course.

Our eyes locked, and it was as if he lured me to him without having to say one word. I make my way over to his section; my eyes gave him a quick scan, which confirmed that he was undoubtedly unavailable. He sat amongst a bunch of vanillas, looking like a chocolate drop, dead smack in the middle. Everything about him was captivating, his eyes, his posture, the way he sat like a boss.

Karina disappeared far too long, so instead of occupying one of the unfilled seats next to him instead of taking this opportunity. I walked right past the VIP section and went to look for my friend. I knew it would only be a matter of time before he'd search for me; they always do. I would be right here waiting when he does.

No sooner than I'd turn the corner, I noticed a group of women huddled in a corner, and Karina was in the middle.

"Why did you bring that black bitch here? We don't need her kind intervening...."

"Never mind that you'd better hope she doesn't manage to get into Sean's section?"

"Who?"

"Sean Hansen," Karina spoke, clearly agitated.

"He would never." Another intervened, waving her hand dismissively.

The fact these women were talking about me and my unwanted presence so freely in front of Karina wasn't the least bit surprising to me. This bitch's whole aura changed talking to these women. Though she didn't have porcelain skin that blended and melded in, she fraternized with them, and more than likely, she longed to be one of them since she was around an adolescent. When I met her, she swore up and down her Icey blue contacts were her natural eyes passed down by her long-lost Irish father.

These racist and envious bitches talking about me didn't move me one bit. I've been getting discussed my whole damn life; when you genuinely don't care what the heck anybody thinks of you, then you reach a dangerously incredible level of freedom. My ass is as free as a bird.

As they whispered amongst one another, I did a quick google search on the name. Low and behold, this man was one I'd been waiting for. Mr. Hansen was a rich, successful brother who was the CEO of his own venture capital company. This man made more money in an hour than I made in two weeks. Not to mention, he was the owner of this gorgeous penthouse we were occupying. Oh, and he had a beautiful wife named Londyn. He was also gorgeous. Did I mention?

"You are too beautiful to be spying, Sweet lady," he said as he entered the room with the dissonance of the guests' conversations following him. I shifted under the weight of his words.

"I wouldn't call it spying. More like investigating all while watching the company you keep."

"That one there, you with her?" He asked, gazing in the direction of Karina.

"Not anymore; I'm with you now." I smiled mischievously. He returned the gesture, and off into the shadows we went.

My ass has been in these shadows now for two years. My phone rang, taking me out of thought and a smile crossed my lips when I saw it was Sean.

"Where are you?" I snapped, remembering how pissed I was.

"Where you want me to be?" A voice answered from behind.

"How long you been fucking her, Sean?"

"What I tell you about questioning me, Danielle?"

Before I could snap at him, he wrapped his arms around my waist, sending shudders throughout my body. He peeled off my robe and bent me over the balcony.

Sean pisses me off more than any other person I've ever met. After only a few months of knowing him, I couldn't get enough of him. I don't know how I even let this go on for so long. The only thing that helps me keep my sanity is that I know with him, I don't have shit to worry about, ever.

Let me just say this, Sean is a satisfying man, had a bitch crying in the bedroom. It was clear why them white bitches were going crazy and why Karina said he was trouble. The man had a chrome penis, okay! A dick that should be shared, hell; you can't be selfish with that monster, it's many women who have never experienced an organism, and I think they deserve to feel and taste this man.

Many men can't handle more than one woman, but Sean, that man can handle, provide for, and dominate team of us effortlessly. He had plenty, but he loved him some me, and I didn't complain because he was not my problem, and I had a plan that would surely backfire.

See, I played my role here because I knew my position, and I've never known him to be sloppy, so why I'd found out from Karina he was fucking with a bitch like Sheila was beyond me. I couldn't grasp the concept of why he'd risked losing me for a scud bucket.

"Why you always gotta be so tough, Danielle? Why can't you just let me love you the way you need to be loved." He hugged me tenderly.

I could feel his girth in my back, and my river began to flow. He knew my weaknesses and played on them. "You know I love you; I give you everything you ask for; I don't give a fuck about Sheila. I fucks her tho, and you gone fuck her with me, ain't you?" he whispers in-between pecks all over my neck.

It was three a.m.; he was supposed to be here at ten. I was tired, but I didn't care. I didn't want to sleep. I liked the ache. I wanted him in me, all of him. I turned to face him and damn near melted in his hands. But then, there she was, Sheila, the nerve of him to bring this bitch to my house.

Remaining calm, my eyes stayed on her, then shifted to him. He walked over to the bed and did that thing he does with his eyes, luring me to come to him. I look back at Sheila as she walks over to me, pulling her shirt above her head. Her body was perfect; she was sexy as fuck.

I stood there frozen. Sheila kissed me in my mouth; her hand gripped my breast as the other parted my legs and rubbed me, hitting my clit, sending shock waves through me. I ran my fingers up and down her back and released her breast from her bra. She panted at my touch, diving deeper into me with her mouth.

"Oh my….". I panted anxiously as an explosive orgasm rocked my body.

Sean lay back and watched the show enjoyingly. "Let's show Danielle what she's been wanting to know. Shall we?"

Sheila pulled me over to Sean, and we both got down on our knees; Sheila wrapped her lips around his dick, she grabbed the base of Sean's dick and guided the rest into her mouth. He braces against the mattress and leans his head back, eyes closed. A moan escapes his lips. He gives in to her.

I intervene as I kiss her lips, take my tongue, and trace slowly from the center of his dick to the tip. Then she uses her tongue to draw circles around the head over and over again. He can barely contain himself with all types of moans and half-spoken profanity coming out of his mouth.

Her lips form a tight grip around the head of his dick, and she slowly sucks, moving her head back and forth. I take him deeper and deeper with each head nod. His hands are tangled into my hair.

She goes back down on me as he starts controlling my head. She takes me in deeper, causing me to take him even more profound and faster. She lifts me and guides me on top of him. I held him and put him in. Taking charge, I held his hands down. He wrapped his lips around my breasts; his lips did something to me.

I went mad; he bucked; he split me in two, freeing his hands from my hold, he pressed me down with one and gripped my neck with the other. Suddenly, he flipped me and took me from behind. I pushed back, forcing more of him into me.

He pulled out and re-inserted himself inside me further and further as his sweat dripped onto my sun-kissed skin. The whole room rocked until the sun came up, and he rocked my body to sleep. I rolled over, opened my eyes, and stared at the space next to me while I ran my hand across the perfectly smooth sheet. I grabbed my phone from the nightstand, checking if Sean's lovely wife had messaged back. But there was nothing.

Deniece Williams, "Silly," serenaded my ears as I was inundated with guilt and regret....

Silly Of me to think that I could ever have you for my guy
How I love you... how I want you...
Silly of me to think that you could ever really want me too
How I love you...

You're just a lover out to score
I know that I should be looking for more
What could it be in you I see

97

TY NESHA

What could it be...
Oh, Love, oh, love, stop making a fool of me
Oh, Love, oh, love, stop making a fool of me
Silly of me to think that you could ever know the things I do
Are all done for you... only for you
Silly of me to take the time to comb my hair and pour the wine
And Know you're not there

You're just a lover out to score
And I know that I should be looking for more
What could it be in you I see
What could it be...
Oh, Love, oh, love, stop making a fool of me
Oh, Love, oh, love, stop making a fool of me

I sighed as I sat up; disappointment coursed through me, and worry settled inside. Since I can remember, I have been exposing men and taking their money. Attempting to expose Sean to his wife might have been a bit much. I'm beginning to realize that I'm spoiled, and I love it. The ring on my finger is a 2-carat princess cut that is my fantasy ring. I have a brand-new car that I got for our anniversary, and I have this big ass house to myself. But something was missing. Him!

I rationalize it because I thought making him match whatever he provided his wife with what he would do for me would be more than enough. But there was this huge void that couldn't be filled with monetary things.

See, the truth is, I never expected to be a starter in this game; I knew what he was capable of and preferred to be on this side of the coin. Lie to that bitch, don't lie to me. I controlled my hand, and it was always on my terms.

Despite what others may think, the side chick is always choosing; the man talks and confides in her. I have always selected my target, and in this game, you must know what type of woman you are.

My first mistake was trusting him. I was a charmer, but he charmed better. He was a seducer, but I had seduced him first. He told me he loved me, and I told him not to be ridiculous; but to be honest,

98

I loved him too.

But love has no room in this game; shit, I don't do love; love is the only emotion that can make you brave, scared, and weak all at once. So, how the hell my icebox melted and my heart reappeared is beyond me. Now I just feel like a piece of shit for feeling this.

I climbed out of bed and headed to the kitchen for a cup of coffee. By the time I made it halfway down, I had heard dishes clattering, and I was excited to know I hadn't been alone after all. But to my surprise, there was another demon I was left to face.

"What the fuck are you doing in my house, and how the hell did you get in?" I snapped in confusion.

"I told you he was trouble, didn't I?"

"What? Karina, what the hell…."

"My brother…trouble!"

"Your brother? Karina, I've been knowing you for over ten years, and I ain't never known you to have a brother. What…

"That's how he prefers it…."

"He? He who."

"You know for such a smart bitch, you dumb. Sean! Daniele. Sean is my older brother."

I wanted to snatch her ass up and drag her all up, and through the very kitchen, she sat in and pretended to care; those nights, I bitched and moaned about him as she extended her fake ass comfort.

"Well, I'll be damned!"

It all was making sense now. The party on Wednesday, her leaving me in the middle of the room alone, as she huddled off with those women and not coming to my defense. He planned this! I thought I was the one choosing the whole time, and he chose me. This mutha….

Before I could respond, someone grabbed me from behind, covering my face with a cloth, sending me straight to slumber.

I awoke in the back of Sean's limo to see him and Sheila staring at me. A bandana was tied inside my mouth, and my hands were bound in front of me.

"The old bitch has awakened." Sheila grimaced.

"I got your bitch!" I murmured through the fabric.

They both laughed uproariously. I clenched my fist as I tried to control my rage.

Sheila crossed her arms, "well, there is no love lost here. I don't like you either. So, you and I have something in common.

The vehicle stopped, and Hector, Sean's driver, opened the door and escorted Sheila out and into another car. He closed the door, and Sean removed the bandana from my mouth.

Tears filled my eyes as I looked him in his. "What the fuck Sean?"

He leaned into me and kissed me on my forehead. "I really loved you, Danny. Karina told me you were damaged goods, but I didn't believe her. The crazy thing is, I trusted you, gave you access to my safe, documents that pertained to my business, shit that could ruin my whole existence. But most of all, I gave you my heart.

I thought I could love you, and my love for *you* would overpower *your* love for money.

I felt that my love for you would subdue your twisted taste for retribution from us, brothas, and I could somehow offset the brokenness you have deep down. But that shit can't be fixed, Danny." He continued, tapping fingers against my chest.

"I loved you, and you tried to expose me with a hundred thousand dollars! Bitch I wipe my ass with that! A tear trickled down his cheek, and the pain in his eyes evince how hurt he was.

My wife didn't and would never respond because she knows who I am, and she doesn't try to change that. She has been here long before you and will remain long after."

He looked down at my feet, and my eyes followed. They were swathed in gold but rather heavy shoes. I couldn't even lift my legs.

The door opened, and Hector dragged me out of the car. I tried to contest and profess my love for him, but it was too late. The damage was done.

The sea of water awaited me, and I already knew what was to come. Sean always told me he wasn't to be fucked with. With him, it had nothing to do with me exposing him and everything to do with respect and trust. I'd lost that. My credit with him was beyond repair, and I could do nothing to fix this debt.

"You wanted the gold, the light, and the power, but you aren't built for the weight that it holds. Now, look at you, with gold cement shoes on." He adorned me with one final kiss and nodded at Hector.

"Dip that bitch!"

Hector tossed me in the pool, and Sean watched in pain as I sank, slowly but surely.

"Hector, let's go to the penthouse; its Wednesday and I need some comfort," Sean ordered before rolling up the window and leaving me drowning in my sorrows.

My cries fell upon deaf ears, and I prayed for mercy and grace but instead, the spirit of The Goddess awaits.

The Goddess

Danielle struggled to stay afloat as she drank her last sip of water.

I leaned over her shaking my head from side to side. "How the hell you ruin good dick cause you in your feelings and oh so greedy, huh?"

I threw my hands up in frustration, "you lost out the moment you thought you could force out his wife, and he would come to you as a constellation prize if you exposed him?

But no, not Danielle. The ungrateful, entitled, stupid brat whenever you didn't get your way. Hasn't anyone told you that you are too damn old to be doing dumb shit? You've been exposing niggas and getting away with it since you were twelve. I bypassed your foolery when you were a young girl, making dumb side bitch decisions. Shit gets old, Danny, and there comes a time when you gotta grow, evolve something!

101

But you can't teach an old dog new tricks, and this time, you ran into a powerful one, and your credit is shot! How the hell did your credit score go from an 800 to a 350? Yo old, tired behind moved from American Express to After-pay trying to gamble in a casino your bank account wasn't set up for.

You can't fuck every nigga the same, and you can't fuck over every nigga the same. You really thought you were going to sell a sex video? Bitch he ain't Ray J, and you ain't Kim! Don't you know that to contract new debts is not the way to pay old ones?"

There ain't enough money in the world that can scare away the dark shadow that looms over your little head. You can't swipe your way out of this one.

Chapter nine, versus 9:1-2, *"The desire of gold is not for gold. It is for the means of independence and benefit. Thy shall not allow one's desires and greed to lead them into bankruptcy."*

Credit Denied.

Sink Bitch SInk!

DAILY READ!

good side chick is the sixth man. Many men get bench players as side chicks and mess around with women with no substance, but a side chick with an agenda is worse. A side chick with a plan has no lines she isn't willing to cross when getting what she wants. She is ready to break up unions, destroy marriages and fight nail and tooth to fulfill her desires.

With the ever-increasing allure and fascination of benefits and perks of the luxurious lifestyle, many women are hopping from one wealthy man to the other as a means to fund a lavish régime. Many will claim that it is fundamentally natural and harmless for women to select their partners based on their ability to provide. They claim that men are perceived as the providers and women as the nurturers in nature and society.

To be frank, gold-digging or the act of dating someone for the benefit of money and/or gifts is considered by some to be a vicious cycle with no end. The "Gold-Digging" side chick asserts that she is no different than the woman those dates for wealth or stature.

To this, I must strongly disagree; some are seeking a deeper intention. In fact, the "gold-digging" side chick has shown just how nasty this cycle can become in the world of *Side Chick Paradise*. She takes full advantage of any opportunity that comes her way to better herself and does not care who she harms to get what she wants.

The gold-digger side chick is one I further advise men not to approach if they have shallow pockets and little gold to mine because she does not spare anyone. If your gold is weak, she does not pity you, and she will dig it and that of your future!

She doesn't have to like him and probably doesn't care about him. Even if she finds a new supply, she still wants to stay connected to him and the benefits of his friendship, so she will do the minimal; a call here, text there, *"just checking in on you, thinking about you,"* etc. But what she is doing is just maintaining a connection when she needs him. He is an ATM; he pays her school fees and buys her clothes. If he offers to pay her off, she will cash out and look for the next ATM. When she empties his bank, the wife will only get air.

This side chick always wants to be number one. She can go diabolical to achieve her aims. She is the one that usually calls the wife to terrorize her. She will manipulate him into spending all his cash on her while giving his wife and kids nothing. Being a side chick that loves the itinerant lifestyle is one thing, but to chase away anything that will risk her having it all. Let alone take desperate measures so that she can take over. She will suck you dry and clean you out unapologetically. Cut her water off and deny her credit, or she will surely destroy yours.

Access Denied!

Side chick affirmation of the day!
Say this aloud and repeat it!

"Patience when you have nothing, Attitude when you have everything."
Side chick-alations
9

LAW TEN

Thou shall not forget their potential

"Comparison is the thief of Joy."
Original copy 10:1

Stormy "The Loveable Side Chick"
How you get em; is how you lose em

"Uh, excuse me? Why are you pushing me to be something I'm not?" Lauryn snapped.

"So, me asking you to show some affection and to come home to a cooked meal ev

ery now and then after work is..."

"Yes, it is! Taking care of your kids is a full-time job, too, you know...."

"I'm so tired of you complaining about doing your job as a wife and handling your womanly duties!"

"See what I mean! He is a sexist; he wants to keep me home barefoot and pregnant, chained to the stove like we still in the 1950s or something."

"I do what I need to do as the man of the house, and all I ask is that you participate, Lauryn."

"Tell her, in what ways, Johnathan." I coached.

"If I'm gone for nine-ten hours out the day, I shouldn't have to ask you to cook and clean; matter of fact, why do I have to come home to a dirty house?"

"You don't wanna come home to a dirty house, cool!" Lauryn stated, throwing up her hands. "Let's air out this 'dirty laundry' that has gone on outside of work hours. How Johnathan here thinks he can go out and have his cake and eat it too. Nah, I'm so tired of his ass."

"Let me ask you this, when and how did you find out Johnathan was having and eating this 'cake.' I rubbed my temples and took a deep breath. Putting my hand up to speak, I parted my mouth and braced myself for the remaining time I had left in this session.

Lauryn crossed her arms across her chest and leaned back onto the sofa. "His little 'whore' messaged me on Facebook, told me EVERYTHING! And I don't know why he even tries to step out; I already told him he ain't gone never keep a woman with that 2-minute dick and all his kids gone have step-daddies cause he ain't shit."

"See what I'm saying? She doesn't respect me, never has. But I bet if I was one of these clowns out here, goin upside her head..."

"I wish thee fawk you would..."

Lauryn and Johnathan had been coming to me for the past eight weeks, and it seemed like a never-ending cycle of a finger-pointing shouting match with no accountability on either end. They have three children, ages 1, 3, and 5. They started like any ordinary couple, fell in love, got married, and had kids. Lauryn dived straight in and immersed herself in the role of mother and wife. Johnathan worked full-time and saw his role as a provider.

I put my hands up to silence them both. I had a migraine and was ready to get this party over with by this time. I managed to maintain my composure and gain back control of the room. "Johnathan, are you willing to share what made you have an affair? What was this other woman doing that you felt you couldn't get from your wife?"

"It wasn't an affair. I never touched the woman. She comes to the coffee shop I use when working out of the office. We talked, and…she grew on me. In a friendly way, though. She encouraged me; she spoke to me like the man I am! She…."

"Man? You ain't no damn man; you are a *boy* in a suit! "Lauryn shouted.

Her insults were always brutal and emasculating; the last time she was here, she told him, *"You act like more of a bitch, than any bitch I know."*

The moment she said it, I immediately felt terrible for him, but she meant it. When I explained to her it was not acceptable in my office to speak to a man or anyone for that matter, in that way, she waved me off and said, *"he just didn't need to push me to the point of actually telling him that."*

Pushing up my glasses, I leaned in towards Lauryn, putting on my stern voice. "Let me first say, Lauryn, I have already told you there would be no name-calling or any level of disrespect tolerated in my office. That's from either of you."

Turning my attention towards Jonathan, I took a breath and spoke; your 'coffee friend' seems nice, but it's pretty clear she has an agenda. Cancel it! It's easy to give support on the sideline when you don't have to deal with the day-to-day struggles of maintaining and holding together a relationship. She was being supportive from afar; that's simple to do when you are not carrying the burden."

I turned my attention back to Lauryn, "an outside person can't break up a solid foundation, and from the looks of it, you seem to be doing a pretty good job of that all by yourself. You two are a team, you are in this together, but Lauryn, it takes two.

Cook this man dinner and clean the house. He isn't asking for much and just hear me out for a second; the way you speak to your man speaks volumes; the disrespect has to end. He is a good man Lauryn, and there are women out there waiting to snag him and cook him whatever meal he wants, ok. He fights with the world out there daily; he doesn't need to come home and fight with the woman he loves, and that he does, sweetie."

"You know what," I stood from my chair and walked over to my bookshelf. "I have a book for you both by an author by the name 'Ty

Nesha.' I have come to love her books, which may have great words of uplifting and encouragement for you, Jonathan.

Lauryn, the book illustrates the importance of uplifting your man, along with the insight on the day-to-day struggles of our black men. She even has prompts that demonstrate by what means to speak to him. *Dear Black King, Can I Fix Your Tilted Crown* and *Dear Black Queen, Step into Your Queendom and Empower your King.*

A book won't fix your issue, though, perchance the best way to begin a dialogue of this magnitude is to clean the slate, stop the blame, and identify the poisonous roots. If you're going to have any chance of getting past your fears, you must acknowledge the embedded stereotypes or negative views you hold. It all starts with you."

I ended my session, thanking the good Lord it was Friday. Marriage counselors aren't magicians. We can't put every relationship back together, and sometimes, we know right away that one isn't going to work. I've learned that one cannot have higher expectations for someone than they have for themselves. And vice versa.

I took a deep breath, picked up my phone, and booked a long overdue session for an evening out with the ladies.

Iwalked into the smoke lounge, and unsurprisingly, my girl Monique was the first one there. Not to mention she was on her second Hookah.

"You good, sis?" I chuckled, sitting next to her.

"I am now." She confirmed, blowing a gust of smoke in the air.

"How is my Godson doing? I need to get over to see him."

"That little negro is being detained in his room until bedtime is officially over."

"What the hell?"

"No, sis, I'm serious."

"What the hell is she yapping about?" Shannon squealed interrupting, Monique's breaking news.

"Well, sis, this story involves a minor, but it sounds like I need to call an attorney for my Godson."

"Did someone say, attorney?" My girl, Love, chimed in, completing our fab four group.

"No, seriously y'all! My son is an almost 2-year-old terrorist! That little fucker held me hostage, dead smack in the restaurant earlier today. And it's important to note the friends I met there do not have children and likely never will. Not, after witnessing this situation first-hand.

We all laughed so damn hard the whole shop wanted in on the tea. One of the girls working in the shop walked over and handed us a bucket of ice and a bottle of my favorite liquor.

I raised my brow in suspicion. "What is…"

"Compliments of the gentleman at the bar." She smiled, handing me a handwritten note while pointing in the direction of the sound of nearby giggling. I looked up from the mysterious letter and came to see a group of girls surrounding him.

"Is that Pa.."

"Patrick Friar!" I scoffed.

"I thought he was..."

"Out of the country… Yea, me too…."

"Well, I knew he was here, Storm."

"Storm" was the name that Monique, my "newscaster" friend, called me when she was tense or mischievous."

"His grandmother told my aunt and…."

"And oh well!" Shannon snapped, seeming more pissed than I was for some reason. But for a good reason.

It was my junior year in college. I was a simple girl with glasses, and everyone found me innocent. None of the boys were interested in me because of my inexperience. The only boy I was interested in was the R&B singer Usher Raymond. I thought I would meet him and fall deep in love one day. But that never happened….

I stayed in my dorm and worked my ass off. But one day, I must have been stressed about something because I wasn't watching where I was going, and I always watched where I was going. But this day, my head was down; I tripped over the damn sidewalk and into the arms of Patrick Friar.

Patrick was the popular one, with all the chicks and thirst buckets multiple breakups because he was not serious about relationships. It was something so familiar about him that I hadn't ever seen before and the first time we were that close to one another. We knew one another from home, but he never paid me any mind. But that day, my heart skipped a beat to a rhythm not even Usher could dance to. I was almost in a fainted condition, and from that day on, we were inseparable. We did everything together -- from taking the same classes, working on projects, exploring campus between classes, and finding part-time jobs.

Until I walked into his dorm room and caught this chick mounted on top of him. I ran out of there so fast that I didn't even see the girl's face. Before I knew it, I heard, from "Monique with the tea." Which was her name at the time. Patrick had been sent out of the country to live with his father, and I never heard from him or saw him again until...

Tonight.

It's been ten years. And here I was frozen, taken hostage by that feeling that I hadn't felt since he'd left. Patrick and I had planned to marry right out of college. It was like a fairy tale. We started dating and fell senselessly in love, so I thought. I swallowed hard as he'd walked in my direction. Before he could reach the table well, my hound dog of a friend, Shannon, stood in-between us.

"It's okay, Shannon, I got this." I stood and faced the giant for the first time, the first man I had loved and the first man to break my heart.

"Well. Look at the time Monique chimed. "Looks like I have to get home, me too, Love seconded.

Well, I got time, Shannon hissed, blowing the smoke from the vape. I raised my eyebrow and gave a head nod clearing her from duty.

"How long have you been here?" I asked, taking a massive gulp from my cup.

"A few weeks." He smiled, watching my every move.

"When are you leaving?"

"You getting rid of me already?" He chuckled.

Silence

111

"I'm not. I have some things. I have some matters to settle, and then I'm here to stay." He said, breaking the silence.

"Why Is that?" I asked. Taking another huge chug from my cup.

There are a lot of factors; aside from me getting a huge offer from my company to relocate; I wanted to feel something familiar again. So, I moved back." He rubbed his hands against his thighs, and there was a brief uncomfortable silence.

"Listen, Mi Mi.."

Mi Mi? I hadn't been called that since Patrick aban...left." I thought.

"I owe you an explanation. I..."

"Was a complete and utter asshole. I thought again.

"We were young and stupid," I said, attempting to shove all the feelings that were suddenly coming back to the surface.

"I wasn't, I knew... I mean, I knew I had something special, and I let it get away from me."

I took another chug from my cup. "Well, I think we all have done some things we regret, but that's in the past now. We are adults. I guess all that matters is the choices we make today." I attempted to take another drink, but Patrick took the cup from my hand.

"I think you have had enough Mi Mi."

There he was again. Calling me a name he has no right to any longer. I don't understand why this is happening to me. I gazed in his direction, and before I knew it, I had downed the whole damn bottle of Dusse' before he could snag that out of my hand. I attempted to stand, but I stumbled and fell into his arms. "Isn't it funny how history repeats itself?" I chuckled, looking into his chestnut brown eyes?

"Let me get you home." He lifted me and cradled me into his arms. I lay my head into his chest as he carried me out and placed me into the passenger side of a brand-new Maserati truck.

"Oh, somebody got a bag, huh?"

"A bag? Where you learn that, Mi Mi?" Patrick laughed, mocking me.

"Forget you, negro!" I sucked my teeth and sassed, adjusting myself into the plush leather seat. "I learned it from my clients. My words slurred.

"Clients. What kind of clients?"

I didn't respond; instead, I gave him my address as I dazed into thought. I rolled down the window and let the cool breeze hit my face. It was a silent drive, and luckily, I lived five minutes from the lounge.

He opened my door, and before I could get one foot out of the door, the liquor and everything else I had inside my stomach landed right on the curb.

Attempting to stand, I stumble. Unsteady on my feet. I must've moved too damn fast because my intoxicated ass fell right into him yet again.

"Come on. Let me get you inside, Mi Mi," he said, in a genuine, caring tone, taking my house keys out of my hand. Before I could say anything, he lifted me up and cradled me in his arms. My head was so heavy I couldn't help laying my head on his rock-hard chest.

Once inside, with every step he took upstairs, I could hear his heartbeat. The rhythm of his heart was all too familiar, giving me the most peaceful feeling I'd ever felt.

"Why'd you even come back? I had already taken responsibility for thinking you were different from the rest and that you didn't love me after all. I had finally come to realize it wasn't enough to turn the page. I must close the whole book. Love sucks! End of story."

<hr>

I woke from my slumber to see Patrick across the room, staring out the dark window. He had on a white wife beater and the black boxer- briefs.

"How long have I been asleep?" I asked sleepily.

"Before or after you cursed me out?" he asked, continuing to stare out the window.

. "Damn. For real?" I questioned, cupping my hand over my mouth.

"Yup. You have been out for a few hours; Shannon somehow

found my number because you weren't answering the phone. I told her you would be up shortly," he explained softly. "She proceeded to tell me that if I touched one hair on your body, she would commence to a whole bunch of shit I refuse to repeat."

By this time, he was standing at the edge of the bed. My eyes scanned his caramel body. He gazed into my eyes, and I could've sworn I had an orgasm right then and there.

"I have something I need to tell you."

Trying to compose myself, I scooched closer to him. I stood up and laid my head on his chest as I did in college. This time, I was a woman, a full-figured woman, not that scrawny petite chick he once knew. I sure as hell hoped he noticed the difference.

"Not now. Don't tell me anything. Just. Just hold me like you used to." I whispered.

I wasn't sure how much longer I could hold back from him, how much longer I could fight the temptation. My inhalation grew heavy as his hands rubbed up and down my arms. Out of nowhere, I softly kissed his chest. He just stood there. So, I kissed it repeatedly. His head slanted back in pleasure, indicating it was okay to proceed. He clasped my abdomen firmly and rubbed his hand up and down each of my rolls and creases. Then he picked me up and placed me on the dresser. Using his body to pry my legs open, he grabbed my hair and tugged it back, kissing me sultrily from my neck down.

"You sure?"

I whimpered my response subtly, wanting him inside of me now.

He posed the question again, this time placing his growing dick against my soaking, purring pussy.

He completed me in every way imaginable, touching parts of my insides I'd forgotten existed. At this moment, he became the conductor and me, his apparatus. He fiddled my violin and stroked every string on my guitar with rhythmic strokes. We intertwined, becoming our own composition as he compelled every key on the ivories. When he deemed it necessary, he even thumped my barrel, drumming into every single part of me. When he wrapped his juicy lips around my flute, I grabbed his head and ran my fingers through his course waves.

He made sure to tend to my every need. He knew exactly what to do to make me forget about everything but the titillating piece of composition he performed on my body as I delivered a sweet, sensual tune of pleasure into his ear. I merited this. I needed him, and today, there was no other place I'd rather be.

I had awoken on a Sunday morning, only to see his eyes fixed on me.

"Thank you for being here for me," I whispered, gazing into his eyes. He rubbed his hands up and down my body; t's like he knew exactly what to do to make me feel good. My body throbbed, but I wouldn't stop him if my life depended on it. Nothing else mattered at this point. I needed one moment amid chaos where I didn't feel the desire to take control and fix everything.

I needed to trust something other than pain, heartache, and the failure of love I had seen in my office time and time again. I was tired of trying to fix everything when I needed a fix deep down inside.

"I'm going to be leaving in a few days. I have some things to tend to," he said, interrupting my thoughts.

"Leaving? I thought…"

"I am; I just have some loose ends to tie up back home, and then you can have me all to yourself." He said, planting a kiss on my forehead.

I turned up my nose, "who said I want that?"

"You want it." He said confidently. "And so do I…."

"Maybe, maybe not." I teased.

"I have something I need to tell you about that day."

"It's in the past. Patrick, I'm over it."

"No, you're not, and neither am I." His voice cracked. "I tried to call you, but…."

"I changed my number; I told all of the girls that if they even spoke of you, I would pour hot grits over them."

"Geesh!"

"Yup." I cleared my throat and felt butterflies in my gut. "But I always knew the years could pass, and if you came running into my arms after all you've done, I would still surround you with my embrace."

Letting the time go, it was already midnight. "Let's talk about it tomorrow evening, at dinner.

"You asking me on a date?"

"I am, I have some meetings and a session tomorrow, but I'll be at your front door at 6 p.m. sharp."

After accepting his offer, we both lay there in silence, not caring about what was. At this very moment, we stayed in the present and wished that time stood still. But life keeps going forward; no matter how much we wish, we can push pause.

The ringing alarm woke me from my dream. I rolled over, looking for Patrick, only to be disappointed... He was gone!

"She gets mad when I hold the door for another woman. She would rather me let it go and allow it to hit them in the face instead".

"You damn right, I am the only woman you should be holding the door for, period!"

I said at my desk and watched for the time. Not even paying attention to the couple that sat before me. This was my last session, and it couldn't go by fast enough. Isn't that something? It's like when you're looking forward to something. Time stands still. But when you're having. Such a good time. You can sneeze. And your time is up.

Just as I was wrapping up, there was a tap at the door.

"Hello, I'm here for my five-o clock session."

"Five, I'm sorry I don't take sessions after 4:30," I stated, looking down at my book. Low and behold, there was a last-minute session that had magically appeared out of thin fucking air. I looked up, and there was one of the most beautiful women standing before me that I had ever seen.

"The secretary, she put me in last minute, I have court tomorrow, and it was a mandate from the judge that we..."

"We?" I said, looking for another body.

"My husband is just parking; he will be up shortly. Do you mind if I use your restroom?"

'Sure, it's down the hall to your left,"

"I am going to kill Brenda," I scoffed. Picking up the phone to call Patrick. Brenda's laughing caught my attention as the familiar voice followed as I dialed his number.

"Right this way Mr....."

"Patrick? How did you know where I work?"

Patrick and Brenda stood in the doorway with puzzled looks on their faces.

"Ah, I see you've met my husband." The lady chimed.

"Your..."

"Yes, my husband. Patrick Friar and I am Jourdan, Jourdan Friar."

I was so unprepared for the stab of misery that was before me. Patrick stays quiet in the face of his truths.

"Mrs. Friar, I noticed there's still some paperwork you needed to complete. Can you just follow me, and we can get that handled for you?"

Brenda knew something was up, and it was a pretty good judgment call on her end.

I took a deep breath and sent a quick text to my partner Kennedy.

"Mi Mi, let me explain."

"Stormy! My name is Stormy!" I snapped. "Matter of fact, it's Ms. Black to you."

"Mi...Storm. Ms. Black. Just hear me out; I can explain all of this." He pleads.

"I don't need to know the plot." I snapped. "I know a married man when I see one." My eyes narrowed as my chest tightened. I could feel the tears ready to assault my restraint.

"There you are!" Jourdan chimed. Her voice became suddenly annoying. "Is everything ok?" She asked, rubbing the side of Patrick's arm.

I took a deep breath, ill-prepared for the stab of misery at the display of gesture, the nostalgia that grew with each gasp. "Oh yes, Mrs. Friar. Everything is wonderful." I lied. "It's just that there was an oversight in the system, and I can't see you two today. Actually ever! I am not accepting any new married couples. But I will have Brenda write you up a letter for court, and I will refer you to my colleague."

"But I was told you are the best."

"Oh, trust me, Kennedy is just as good, if not better."

"Speaking of." Kennedy appeared in perfect time, rescuing me from this nightmare unfolding before me.

Patrick tried to get my attention, but I refused to look up. I lingered impatiently for them to exit out of my office. Brenda closed the door behind them, and I collapsed on the couch, rummaging for a liberator in this unforeseen calamity.

"What the hell was that?" Brenda asked, sitting next to me, throwing her arm over my shoulder.

"That was...my heart being yanked out of my chest is what that was. I cant..."

"Wait! Shhhh." She interrupted as she cupped her ear and leaned into the wall. "You hear that? Listen..."

`The walls were thin, and we couldn't hear Jourdan and Patrick on the other side.

The way she spoke to him was horrid. She was so beautiful; I'd never expected such nasty things to come out of her pretty little lips. We leaned into the walls to get a better listen, and before we knew it, there was a large thud, and my door busted wide open, startling us both. Brenda and I tried to disguise our acts, but we were caught.

"Mmmh, hmm, I knew you nosey heifers were eavesdropping." Kennedy poked her head out the door and looked around before coming back into the office closing the door behind.

That is a hot mess!" she uncovered. Pointing out the door and shaking her head. "Apparently, they have been married for ten years..."

My heart sank at the revelation.

"But there's a back story." She continued. There was a brief moment of silence be for she spoke again. "But I think you should hear it from him."

I glanced up in uncertainty as she opened the door. Patrick was standing on the other side.

Before I could rebuttal, Kennedy put her hand up to silence me. "Storm, he didn't tell me, I figured it out, and you need to hear this!" She said sternly, not taking no for an answer.

It was uncomfortable, he and I alone in this office after the gut-wrenching way we'd had it out earlier. There was a bit of relief in knowing there was a story behind the marriage and how it trails back to Patrick leaving me behind in college. I shudder beneath his gaze.

He parts his mouth to speak. "This wasn't my idea."

"Is it true? I ask." Questioning him like he's a criminal. I bite my lower lip and steal a glance.

He walked over and sat across from me. This was unusual, me on the couch as he sat in my seat. He took a breath and looked into the air as if he were in deep thought. "I was at my desk as I studied for the next day's exam. I heard a tap at the door, and I thought, it was you; I walked over and opened the door, not even bothering to look up. She jumped on me in excitement, catching me by surprise as I fell to the bed. I heard sniffles and feet running away, but her father and my father appeared at my door before I could process it all.

"Jourdan was a model that I met in Paris when I visited my dad two months before you and I started dating. They had come to tell me she was pregnant, and my dad was disenrolling me from school." He leaned over and rested his chin into his hands, "there was a shotgun wedding the next week."

"So, you have kids?"

"Twins, but they are only five. She lied. She was never pregnant. In fact, she was on the pill. By the time I figured it out, it was too late. Due to our culture and beliefs, there was no such thing as divorce. But my father passed a year ago, and tired of living in his shadow, and up to his expectations, I filed for divorce a month ago. Soon as I filed. I decided I would come for you, Stormy. I wanted to tell you, but...."

That's when it happens, the little moment of grace that can descend suddenly to signal the end of a fight. My sulk sways a little. I felt the muscles between my shoulder blades loosen, my turning stomach ease. And at the same time, I couldn't deny the other thing; I was feeling butterflies. Deep in my stomach, down between my legs, even while we talked about how this would pan out moving forward.

Six months later...

I tried swallowing the lump in my throat, but my mouth was too dry. My eyes were closed, but in my head, I knew what had to be done. My move was to leave Chicago and never return. My eyes flutter as I lay there on my back. He should be lying here next to me, but instead, he was walking out the door. He was a good man, and my time spent with him was coming to an end.

What was this I was feeling? How did I let it get to this point? Tears pricked the corner of my eyes. I'm a damn marriage counselor, for Pete's sake; my skin should be thicker by now! But how is it possible not to feel the way I did when the one you thought was your true love was on the verge of walking out on you?

A month after Patrick's divorce, things between him and I shifted from sugar to shit. Jourdan found out about Patrick and me and went on a rampage. She began to blame me and proceeded to call me a homewrecker. She attempted to sue me and my practice for conflict of interest and left nasty remarks on my website. I had even gone as far as accusing Patrick of still sleeping with her. I was not convinced that she calls all hours of the night, and he jumps when she calls.

One day I even took it upon myself to reach out to her and come to an understanding. But she was unwilling to do so. "You are a marriage counselor that is supposed to save marriages, yet you chose

120

to date my man and break up a marriage." She chuckled. "But let me tell you what your future will look like. I am wife number one; you can only aim to be wife number two. My ex-husband, I are friends. We call and text on occasion about the kids or other situations we were never again romantic, thanks to you! But not in your distrustful mind. You don't like us talking; it makes you feel uncomfortable, not my problem!"

She hung up the phone and blocked my number. What she was saying wasn't true at all. I had no part in breaking up their marriage. It was Patrick's own free will. She would say these things to guilt trip me and make herself feel better. Her twisted mind infuriated me. Jourdan liked to play mind games, projecting, and shit, and I must admit, it worked. No matter how far Patrick would bend to show me there was nothing between the two of them, I refused to believe him.

I fought with him and stopped sleeping because my self-esteem had gotten low as I compared my plus-size figure to the size six-figure of Jourdan. I would beat myself over the head with the mantra society speaks of, "how you get 'em is how you lose 'em." Even though I always told my clients that cheating and being a cheater are not the same. Cheating is an act of flesh that no one is exempt from; a cheater is a person that chooses to continue the action repeatedly. That's my motto.

Yet, I lost myself in insecurities and became the very woman I advised my clients not to become. Eventually, I got away from what it was we had.

I walked out to his balcony, "Siri play "Kelly Price," *As We Lay*. I love this song. I played this song repeatedly whenever Patrick had to go back home to Jourdan before the divorce.

As we lay
Didn't think about
The price we'd have to pay
No, no, no

It's morning
And now it's time for us to say goodbye
Goodbye baby

TY NESHA

You're leaving me
I know you've got to hurry home to face your wife, wife

I would never want to hurt her, no, no, no
She would never understand
You belong to me for just one night
As we slept the night away

I let the words to the song serenade my ears as I thought back to our morning conversation,

"I'm tired of having this conversation, Stormy. You keep delving into her twisted game, and you will hurt your own feelings. Jourdan has a dark side Stormy and right now, her ego is severely bruised. She will tell you anything that she can to make you feel like there's something more going on that there isn't. That's her reality, not mine!"

He began to pack a bag, and I tried to snatch it out of his hand. He pulled it away as his eyes looked briefly surprised before they narrowed. "Who are you? Did you forget? You were never this way, ever! You need to get your head back right and stop allowing Jourdan the power over you. I'm tired; I can't keep doing this." He said, throwing his hands up. "Going back-and-forth, it's becoming stressful. I can't do the drama. I require peace. I didn't leave a draining marriage to enter a union with the love of my and...."

"I need my peace, and I won't compromise that for Jourdan or anyone else, not even you. Something shifted, Patrick's face goes empty as if interest has exhausted right out; he zips his bag and throws it over his shoulder. I don't try to stop him.

I peer out at the view and recollect my thoughts. I had finally realized what I had done here and decided to call Patrick and apologize. I picked up my phone to a plethora of notifications,

Pat: I can't do it anymore, Stormy. I loved you, and I tried my absolute best to show you the love you deserved. You chose to try to pick fights with me. I never responded. You will accept me for who I am and love me will be my happily ever after. But deep down. That's not how our story would end. This was a mistake; I'm going back home to Jourdan.

122

My heart dropped at his message, I picked up the phone to call him, but I felt a stab of pain in my right shoulder.

"You were nothing more to me than an unqualified woman who dated a married man, all because you had no self-worth! You were fucking my husband far before the ink dried on the divorce papers! That makes you a homewrecking bitch."

Jourdan had stabbed me! Behind my back at that.

I gasped for air as I turned swiftly; before she could bring the knife down on me again, I grabbed her arm, and out of nowhere, Patrick's phone dropped out of her jacket as I realized now, who had sent that last message as we struggled over the balcony.

I kneed her as hard as I could in her gut and grasped her shoulders, pulling her in toward me as I gave her a stiff head butt. She slumped over, dropping the knife, and I kicked it off the balcony.

Gripping her hair, I yanked her head back. I used my other hand to stroke her face as if offering some gesture of solace. "Shhh, it's ok. I know you had no clue who you were fucking with. Unfortunately, you fucked with the wrong bitch." I grimaced before rocking her whole body with a blow to the face. "Your home was broken far before I started fucking your *ex*-husband." I hissed before banging her head against the banister, knocking her unconscious.

I picked up the phone and took a breath leaning over the balcony to keep my balance.

"911, what's your emergency?"

Before I could speak, I felt a rush against my body as I went flying over the terrace, sending me crashing onto the sidewalk.

Goddess

"I'd seen this movie before. This time you're being called to a moment of reflection. There I was, all caught up in your limelight; you two were in love, indeed! You both had me cheering on the sidelines as he swept you off your feet, did the most romantic things like uttered the cutest nothings in your ear; adorable, no– really, it was.

He was readily available exhibited no signs of wanting to be covert. A rock-solid on your way to the chantry of love, type bond. A break the bank to pay for the 'wedding of the year' type relationship. You finally reach the objective of being the prototypical happily ever after Cinderella and Prince Charming couple.

And over time, everything…disintegrated.

Goddammit!

When you allow another individual the power and control over you, you have already lost the battle and that you did. Jourdan was rotten, and Patrick didn't want any parts of her, and you allowed her to make you wretched. He grew tired of your despair, and I can't say I blame him. You began to self-sabotage and made everything a self-fulfilling prophecy.

The funny thing is, the simple yet sincere act of holding the mirror up to yourself can truly be a frightening experience. As if you're seeing yourself through your own new eyes.

While most parts may seem familiar, you notice new things about yourself that are unrecognizable, utterly foreign, and make you feel like you started staring at a stranger.

Since you have issues with strength, do you want to borrow my balls for a while until you get it right? Need I remind you of, **Original copy of 10:1.** *One thing you did was fall into envy and comparison and forget who the fuck you were! Comparison is the thief of Joy. You are no one's carbon copy."*

Patrick and Jourdan's relationship was built on a lie from the jump. The lie was not his. Patrick remained loyal to a situation based on false expectations from outside parties. When he finally decided to put himself first. He chose love; he chose you.

He was a man with integrity and character who could provide, protect and build; build a fire without a match. A man that honored Divinity and his decrees. Most of all, a man that did what had to be done to be successful in life without compromising principles or character.

Before this, you needed no one's acceptance; comfortable in your skin. You allowed insecurities and a "homemade" mantra (how you get em, is how you lose 'em) created to make the other woman feel better about her cheating spouse, to intervene in a solid foundation.

See, a friend ignores your broken fence and appreciates the flowers in your garden. But too bad I am not your friend; It's the discomfort and failure that teaches you the best lesson in life and provokes you to restore yourself and stand again with a firm conviction. You wanted the smoke, and you lit this fire. Now it's time....

Burn in Hell!"

DAILY READ!

eople have this huge misconception: If your partner has cheated dating you while in a relationship, what makes you think he won't do the same thing to you?

I've witnessed firsthand people that's cheated on their girlfriend with their current wife. I've also seen men who courted their current girlfriend or wife away from her now ex-boyfriend. I've never seen a relationship last very long if it doesn't evolve. Evolution is the secret to the next step.

I knew a guy in a loveless marriage; he didn't look to go out and cheat. He wanted a divorce; she didn't. He sought counseling, reached out for advice, and tried to work things out. He was no longer happy. He met someone; by then, the marriage was over, they slept in separate rooms, and the sex was almost non-existent.

As his friendship blossomed with the woman, he grew distant. He never cheated, but they were done at the end of his marriage, and he was with someone else for two years before his divorce was settled.

Five years later, they have been doing just fine. No trust issues because there was always honesty. There is no fighting or drama; it's not perfect, but what is? Not one time has anything ever indicated trouble thus far.

Will they last forever? Only time will tell.

We have been taught through old-fashioned wisdom *"that the way you get him is the way you'll lose him."* However, let's look at it through another lens; the way you get him is rarely the way you keep him.

When we assume "once a cheater, always a cheater," we deeply underestimate people's ability to change.

The truth is, it's all fair in love and war.

As I stated earlier, many factors play a role in cheating. However, as hard as may be to digest this, the bitter truth is a man doesn't leave his current partner for another woman. He goes because he has been unhappy for quite some time.

The other woman demonstrates that he doesn't have to be despondent anymore. He is leaving for himself. There wouldn't even be another woman if he was happy in his relationship unless he is just one that spontaneously requires multiple partners.

People assume that meeting someone in such a manner is destined to fail. However, this is so far from the truth. If the person that stepped out was sincere and felt compelled to stay in a relationship they didn't want but innocently fell for someone else, what difference would it make? It is an entirely different narrative if he wanted his cake and ate it too and is just a serial cheater.

The chances of it lasting are no different from any other relationship. People meet, date, have lust, love, etc. all people are different. Some grow together, and some grow apart just because he met someone while in a relationship does not change the chances of success. Unless the person they cheated with becomes a different person.

Just an observation from someone who has seen this scenario occur firsthand. When you are a side chick that moves up as the primary/only or whatever you want to call it, you must never forget your partner has left their significant other for a reason. There could be many reasons for this.

You have to use discernment and know who your partner is. Sometimes we get hung up on old wives' tales and many churchy references and allow that to cloud what is right in front of us. Know who you are and stop letting what other people say to feel superior cause you to lose yourself. Their perception doesn't have to be your reality.

Side chick affirmation of the day!
Say this aloud and repeat it!

All is Fair in Love and War
Side chick-alations
10

EPILOGUE

laying the game is one thing; following the rules to the game is another. The thing is, inside *Side Chick Paradise,* the longer you stay, the more complex it is to play by the rules.

However, this book has explained the dirty details of what to expect when these rules are broken. There are levels to this, and it is not for the faint. Cheating always includes secrets, drama, and lying, so a side chick must follow the rules to avoid trouble.

A true side chick has her motive, and she doesn't want the stress and bullshit that comes behind *his* cheating ass. Sometimes, she's getting over or through her own discrepancies. All she wants is the benefits and the pay; you can keep the extra sauce.

On top of this, she is going to get you right. She won't nag, blow up your phone, question, or get all up in your "space." Because there isn't any drama, she offers peace of mind and sanity and gives you the pleasure you wouldn't imagine.

The danger behind this is that *he* wants to spend more time with her, and the closer they get, the closer the feelings develop, and this is where shit gets real. The plot thickens.

Now again, I'm not promoting side chicks; they have been around far before I was conceived. However, I was indeed "The Successful" one back in the day.

Hell no! I ain't sorry!

I was dealing with my own shit, but baby, his sorry ass was in heaven breaking all the rules, and I had to cut him off. To this day, he says I should've been his wife, tells my friends, his friends, and I know he means it because…

I hit 'em with that "side chick" love.

But it's different today; there are no rules or boundaries in place, especially with social media. The truth is, being a side chick isn't for everyone.

Do you think you have what it takes?

This book has explained the dirty details of what to expect when these rules are broken. There are levels to this, but once you knowingly become the "other woman," you enter the "Sidepiece Agreement," you must fully understand and abide by the terms of the deal, and if you don't, well, there is a price that must be paid.

For if the laws are broken, thou shall burn in the pits of side chick hell. Ashes to ashes, dust to unruly side chicks."

Pidd Poo!

To be continued!

10 LAWS OF A "MAIN CHICK."
If You Can't Stand the Heat, Get The Hell Out The Kitchen

The Goddess Returns!

If you women are waiting on some magical sisterhood to end a cheating man's shenanigans then, you're delusional. The fact that the term "homewrecker" exists proves that you need to recognize that many women don't want to leave their dilly-dallying partners, nor want to blame them. There's never any energy pointed towards side men. Why?

Many men risk cheating because it's a nonsensical concept. After all, a big part of the blame is pushed up on the side chick. They take the risk because they are often forgiven for stepping out, and if they still have the side chick as an option, they can't lose. With this, this is precisely why women are out here, requiring loyalty from one another as the men are out here frolicking in strains of the yoni.

I've been the woman who was cheated on and the woman who a married man approached. One thing that I've always found to be shared was a man who was either unhappy at home, unmindful of his wife, unsatisfied in his relationship, or just damn selfish!

Either way, it's him!

He made that vow, and he decided to break it. For some reason, women believe he won't cheat if he doesn't have anybody to fool with. That doesn't mean he'll be a good boyfriend or husband. There are so many reasons why men and women cheat. They all are a choice. Figure out why that's the choice instead of blaming someone outside of the relationship.

I may step on a few toes here, but I'm going to be honest; If you aren't my friend, family, or someone I am close with, you owe me nothing! Why get mad at the next chick and gain another enemy just to repeat the same cycle?

Why get all worked up if you keep accepting the bull crap?

A woman those sleeps with another woman's man is no less than the woman that takes him back. She may have known you were in a relationship, but so did he! If she has low self-esteem for sleeping with him, you have low self-esteem for taking him back, period!

If you are "bad," remove yourself from the table, rather than believing you are better the main vs. the side…. either way, both are feeding him; you can't change him, but you can remove the table.

Starve his ass or let him cheat in peace!

CHECK YO MAN! Or the Goddess will surely come to check you!

LAW ONE

Thou Shall Get up From the Table
"You are the table!"
Starve his ass 1:

Jay "The "Enough is Enough" Main Chick"
What's Done in the Dark

sat at the edge of my bed, hoping and praying what I had just seen all over the media was just a dream, hell a nightmare in this case. I mean, Rodger has made some sick mess but, this?

"Jay! My sister came rushing in with her two minions behind. Oh, my goodness, baby, are you ok?"

"That is some messed up shit Jay....and the Hoe talking about a baby!"

My head jolted up, and my heart dropped to my shoes yet again.

"Tracy, I told you not to...."

"Baby? Are you? Wait! What do you mean you told her not to Kim? Why in the hell is she yelling out some shit that should have come first hand from you?"

"Jay, Tracy told me on the way, and I told her to let me..."

My sister's eyes darted over to her girl with a look of death.

"Sis, that's the least of your worries right now..." Lacey shrieked, turning up the volume to the television.

"The mistress of Rodger Davis, Ceo of Atlanta's largest entertainment Lawfirm, has confirmed the allegations of a pregnancy and a secret two-year-old son."

From there I heard nothing, I saw nothing, my world shattered right there, my life, my home everything had just been destroyed right in front of the whole damn world; and there ain't a departmental unit in this world that could put out the flames I'm about to bring...

Count your days Rodger, I'm about to introduce you to hell!